Antlers of Bone

Taylor Denton

Published in North America and Europe by Running Wild Press. Visit
Running Wild Press at www.runningwildpress.com Educators, librarians,
book clubs (as well as the eternally curious), go to
www.runningwildpress.com.

ISBN (pbk) 978-1-947041-96-7
ISBN (ebook) 978-1-955062-00-8

For my mother and father

Trigger Warning:
The following story contains images of self harm
and attempted suicide.

Chapter 1
The Present, Beginning

Lily always knew she would become a stag after she died. When she was a child, her every fantasy was of her decomposing corpse as the Earth sucked it down into the dirt. She would imagine her body being absorbed into the soil. Her hair would melt away into the grass. Her eyes would sit in the bellies of crows as they flew to nest in mountain trees. Then, from that decay, a stag would rise with antlers like long fingers reaching upwards toward the sun. Finally, she would find silence.

"You'll love this place, Lily," Maggie said, the tight smile against her lips made her voice sound restrained. "I've read so many great things. I think Lindsay Lohan even stayed there for a while."

Lily stared out the window with her forehead pressed against the glass.

"They have a great program there. They even have horses, you loved horses when you were little."

Lily turned to look at her sister. She kept her body slouched against the passenger side door. Her arms were wrapped around her middle as she watched Maggie tighten her hands on the wheel.

"I don't feel right," Lily finally said. "I want to go home."

Her words sounded strange to her. It was as though her voice had not been used in weeks, and she was only just beginning to break it in again. Had she ever spoken at all? Her head burned, her body ached, and she felt as though she was consumed by a fever.

Maggie kept her eyes fixed on the road. "No. Nope. You know we can't. Dr. Lomax says that isn't going to work. He's known you since you were little, we can trust him on this."

Lily's fingers ran through the follicles of her mulberry sweater. Her heart pounded and a lump lodged in her throat. Her eyelids twitched as she watched her sister.

"How long?" she asked.

Maggie's brow furrowed. "Hmm?"

Lily felt a scream as it struggled to free itself from her chest. "How long will I have to stay?"

"We've been through this. I don't know. That'll be up to your doctor."

Lily's bottom lip quivered. She looked back out toward the open sky. The front windshield served as a barrier between her and the infinite musky grey-blue. She reached her fingertips out to rest against the glass.

"You've got to be reasonable about this," her sister said. "I can't take much more. And I can't keep missing work because of you. Mom and dad are at their breaking point. Something … something needs to give."

At home, Lily had always imagined herself fading into the pastel floral wallpaper, which had been plastered throughout their farmhouse. Her childhood and early adolescence were blurred for her, as though all of her twenty-one years were spent waking up from a dream and falling back into slumber simultaneously. Is that what she wished for? Was she grateful?

"Prison," Lily whispered.

"No, it's not, for God-sakes. You can leave any time you like, there's nothing legally binding you to stay. I've told you all this already."

"You'll forget about me. I'm disappearing, Maggie."

"Stop it."

"I'm disappearing. Can you even see me anymore?"

"You're being melodramatic again."

"I want you to look at me," Lily said, not making a move to straighten out her body.

"What? No, I'm watching the road. I'd like to survive the trip there."

Lily's hands tingled with the desire to wrap themselves around her sister's neck. She pressed her finger down to roll the window open. Wind gushed into the car. She closed her eyes, her lips parting as air flowed out of her lungs. Her hair whipped behind her, the weight of it lifted away from her back.

"Jesus, Lily. Pull your hair back, it's hitting me in the face."

Lily moved her hands from the interior of the car, keeping her eyelids shut. She felt herself rise, her thin sweatpants peeled away from the leather seat. She hovered in mid-air, floating. She did not exist for a moment. She did not belong.

"You've got to believe me. This is for the best. Don't you want to get better?"

Lily collapsed back onto the vehicle's interior. Gravity had its hold on her again.

"I want to go home," she said.

"All I've heard you talk about for the past ten years has been moving away, leaving the farm. Now all you want is to go back. That's very *you.*"

Lily opened her eyes. Her hair sliced into her face and barred her from having a clear view of the outside. She felt illness unsettle her interior, churn and burn the inside of her again. She looked at Maggie. She was beautiful. Her sister was stunning. Maggie was perfection in all of her school portraits. Maggie sang for the church choir. Maggie knew when to smile when someone spoke to her. Maggie did not have a temper.

"Can you see me? Can you see me at all?"

Maggie's grip on the wheel relaxed. She cocked her head to the side, reluctantly focusing her gaze on her sister.

"Lily…I -"

A movement caught Lily's eye, a brown flash that leaped out in front of the car. Her instincts took over before her mind had the chance to process what she saw.

"Maggie!" She threw her arm out in front of her sister.

Lily saw her foot slam against the break. The car skidded against the black asphalt, swerving as it ground to a halt. The front bumper knocked lightly against a stag as it frantically rushed across the road, its hooves danced as it tripped across the street.

"Fuck, I think we hit it," Maggie said. "Is it hurt?"

Lily did not answer. She watched the stag. Its eyes darted around wildly until they landed on her's. Lily's soul lurched, and her breath shuddered.

She saw his eyes flushed with a savage, primitive panic. It was frenzied and made his iris glow bright. His chest heaved in and out furiously, breath came in white puffs; vapors which dissipated into the iced air.

Lily's hand flew down to the handle of the passenger seat door. She flung the door open, throwing her body outside.

"What in the hell? Get back in the car, you'll freak it out," Maggie said.

The stag's eyes remained on Lily, who watched as frantic clouds emanated from the stag's nose, hanging in the air. The wind blew her hair back behind her in a curtain. She listened as the Earth stilled. The stag turned into a statue, fixed in place from terror. Lily knew that they had suspended time. They had stopped the world from spinning. She was aware that they were alive only because of the stag's breath. She shifted her foot, attempting to move closer to him. The stag's hooves clicked against the asphalt as he turned, taking off into the surrounding field.

"What did you think was going to happen?" Maggie said. "Get back in the car, we're going to be late."

Lily glanced downward, falling back into the vehicle. Lily could not afford to exist. She was a curse.

"I'm so tired," Lily said.

She saw Maggie's eyes flutter shut for just a moment.

"Me too," her sister muttered.

Lily had always been envious of her sister's freckles, her tawny brown hair, her small nose, and thin lips. Her sister was solid, firm, her presence deeply rooted. Maggie looked real. Maggie knew that she was real. Lily scanned her, moving her fingertips to rest against her pale, freckled arm. Maggie flinched away, her muscles clenched against Lily's touch.

"Don't forget about me," Lily whispered.

What did she want? Did she want to exist? Did she want to disappear? Perhaps all of her twenty-one years were leading up to this, to Meadowlark.

Maggie laughed. "You're always melodramatic."

Lily closed her eyes, shifting her body to rest her head against Maggie's shoulder.

"I'm disappearing, and everyone is about to forget that I was ever there." She was unsure whether she was lamenting or reflecting. Meadowlark would be her judge.

"So melodramatic."

***

"Meadowlark Farm is different from any other mental facility," the doctor said. "We pride ourselves on giving our patients a truly unique therapeutic experience."

Maggie nodded, her hands rested on her lap. "Yeah, absolutely. I've done so much research on this place and I've heard nothing but really fantastic things."

The doctor straightened his back. "That's great to hear."

Lily stood near the window. Her arms crossed over her chest as she watched the two of them speak. Maggie sat perched at the front of the doctor's desk while he stared at her. Neither of them paid attention to Lily.

"I know that my sister was concerned about her freedom here. She has a difficult time with confinement." Maggie said.

"We want our patients to feel like they are in control of their time at Meadowlark. What happens here will be up to her."

Lily furrowed her brow. He had not answered the question.

"That's good, that's good. We were also wondering about the timeline. How long do you imagine her stay will be?"

"Again, that'll depend on her. Our goal is to allow the patient to chart their own treatment. We want to have her back to you and your family as soon as possible. I imagine you know of the 'Right to be Well' law which was passed just a few years ago."

Maggie fidgeted in her seat. "I think I may have heard of it on the news once or twice, but it's been a while. Would you mind refreshing me?"

He leaned forward on his desk. "Yes, of course. A landmark ruling, led by the Republican party. In short, the 'Right to be Well' law takes away any government involvement in certain institutions, such as mental facilities. It essentially means that places like Meadowlark can function independently of any rules or regulations. Treatment can be whatever we want it to be."

"Ah, yeah, okay. I do remember that, as a matter of fact. My whole family are proud Republicans, except for Lily, of course. She all but vomits at the mention of the word," Maggie said.

"We'll just have to fix that too, won't we?"

They both began to laugh.

Lily bit her lip. She imagined taking a glass-blown paperweight down on his head. She pictured the blood that would burst from his balding skull. She spun on her heels to look out the window. She took a slow breath inward, holding it there.

"My mother was worried about supervision," Lily heard Maggie continue. "Especially in the shower and the bath."

Lily listened for his response. Finally, he replied. "There was a suicide attempt on December 3rd in a bathtub, is that correct?"

She heard a shuffle behind her, and Maggie cleared her throat. "That's right."

"Alright," he said. His voice had softened. "We'll make sure to take the necessary precautions."

Lily bent her head forward. Her hair fell over her face. She kept her eyes fixed on the window. She was unsure where she was. The hills and flowered meadows told her that it was the country up in the mountains. Some trails led into a ring of trees that surrounded the facility, a lovely cage. Pools of gardens were scattered all across the field and brimmed with colors that felt unnatural for the winter. Horses wandered across the pasture, some mounted by riders and some not. She felt as though she gazed into a perpetual painting.

"Lily?" The doctor's voice called softly. "Would you like to look around the place a little? I know you haven't been given a tour yet."

Lily was shocked to hear him speak her name. The soundwaves materialized to form the words proved that he could see her. She did not know how to respond.

Maggie snapped her fingers in her direction. "Don't be rude. Answer him."

"No, it's alright. This is a process, it takes time," he replied.

There was silence for a moment. Lily's head began to ache. Footsteps echoed through the room, near her. She felt his warmth as he came closer to her.

"We have your room all set up. I'd like to show you and your sister around, what do you say?"

She shivered as the doctor breathed on her neck. She moved closer to the window to put some distance between them.

"She's not much of a talker," Maggie said. "She didn't even speak her first word until she was ten. And she doesn't like people getting close to her."

"It's a process. Let's just let her follow behind us. She'll catch up when she wants to."

Lily moved her head so her hair fell against her back and away from her shoulders. She didn't want to be alone in that room any longer. She followed behind Maggie and the doctor, while keeping significant space between them.

"One thing that's important to us here is making sure our patients have their own space and privacy, but we encourage roommates to keep everyone social. With Lily, we've opted to ..."

Lily lost track of their voices as she looked around the halls. The floors were lined with tile, pristine white. She could very nearly feel the texture through her thin sneakers. The walls were lined with excessive art, mostly Van Gogh. She could not help but wonder what effect they were trying to elicit. It was almost as if they were trying to say, 'See? Even crazy people who cut off their ear can be successful. Even if that success doesn't arrive until after you've shot yourself and your carcass is deteriorating in the ground.'

"We have a great number of activities for the patients to try. We have a gym that some of our patients use as a dance studio. Your sister is a dancer, is that correct?" Lily heard him ask.

Maggie's gaze turned to him.

Lily waited, curious as to what she would say in response.

"She used to be."

Her sister's answer hit her in the stomach and knocked all the air from her in a hard stroke. She stumbled a little but kept her balance and continued to follow behind them.

"That's right. Perhaps she'll find her new passion here. We have a painting class, a cooking class, a common room for our patients to watch films; we find it does wonders for a patient's morale. And we encourage the family to leave them some spending money, if they're good sometimes we order take-out for group dinners."

"That sounds great. But to be frank, she's not the most sociable. We live on a chicken farm, and she likes spending time with them more than us. One of the main reasons I chose this place was because of the thing you guys do with horses."

"The Equestrian Therapeutic Contact Program. That's my absolute favorite. We match up a patient with a volunteer here in the community who's a trained rider, and they teach them how to handle a horse. They take them on trips through pathways in the fields. It helps our patients get fresh air, it forms a bond between human and horse, and sometimes a friendship even develops between the volunteer and patient. There are no downsides."

"That sounds perfect. I know she'll love that."

"Indeed, indeed."

The doctor and Maggie continued to talk idly as Lily followed. The three of them walked into a separate area of the facility, a large room where Lily saw other humans for the first time since her arrival at Meadowlark. The furniture was minimalistic and simple, mostly whites and blacks. No greys. The walls were painted a bright white that stung her eyes. *Rhapsody in Blue* played softly through the speakers.

"This is the common room I mentioned, a favorite spot for our patients. We have board games, television, regulated of course, and it's a great place for them to interact with one another."

Lily examined the other patients. She tried to look at their eyes.

"We encourage our patients to come here after therapy. It offers a nice place to relax and unwind."

They all seemed wearied. Some were exhausted in a relieved sort of way; others were simply worn down from a force that no one else could see. She wondered if they could see her. She wondered if they noticed her staring.

"I hear it will snow tomorrow. The patients should enjoy that. These cathedral-style windows give them a great view of the outside."

She could not reach them and they could not reach her. She looked to the right and there she saw a man wear a royal purple shirt that was big on him. His feathery curls were coal-black. They were a deeper ebony than the sky at night. He was pale and he held his chin in his hand. His body leaned back against a white chair with sharp edges. It hardly seemed comfortable.

Lily's steps slowed as she watched him. He was absorbed in a novel, not noticing her. She continued to stare, her arms dangled at her sides. Something about him fascinated her, mesmerized her. He was too thin, too white, and too delicate. His gaze flicked up from his book.

His eyes were a darker blue than her's. He took a deep breath inward, then let it out. He shifted slightly in his chair, looked away from her to concentrate on his reading. A shiver traveled down her spine, and she quickly turned away.

He had seen her.

"Let's take you to Lily's room. No doubt you'll want to see your sister's new home."

Lily bit her lip. There was a prick, and blood trickled down and onto her tongue. She sucked her lip into her mouth. They continued to walk while her eyes remained downcast on the tile.

"All you have to do is round this corner, and you get to Lily's wing. She will have a wonderful view."

"And what wing is this exactly?" Maggie asked. "You mentioned 'Lily's wing,' what wing would that be?"

Lily watched as the doctor flipped his head to look at her sister. His voice grew quiet as he replied, "The Anger Management wing."

"That's fine, totally fine. But, I mean, that's not why I brought her here. I brought her here because ... because of what happened on December third and I thought I explained this."

She saw his fingers laced together. "Yes, I understand. In truth, the wing does not make much of a difference. The treatment is still very much personalized. It's a process, you know."

"I just want to make sure that our money is going to be spent on something that'll fix her. I promised my parents that this wouldn't be a waste." Maggie's tone grew more irritated.

Lily blinked. Her lips parted.

The doctor adjusted his glasses and shifted uncomfortably. "Margaret, I assure you, Meadowlark is a healing place. We foster mental health in a wide variety of ways. Your sister will be in good hands; this I can promise."

Lily noticed that his voice was all but mechanical, robotic. He sounded like a recording. She looked to the tile again. Her sister's black shoes entered her line of vision. She did not look up. The shoes stayed still for a moment, then cheated to the right.

"She's very specific about what she wears. She can't do jeans, can't do yoga pants, even. All she'll wear are those sweats. They need to be washed once a week. Do it at night, when she's in her pajamas. I like to do it on Saturdays, but I'll leave that up to you, obviously. She has five T-shirts that she'll wear. I've packed all those. And this God-awful sweater." Her voice began to break. "She all but sleeps in this. It can't go in a dryer. It'll have to air dry. Do you understand? She'd freak out if it shrunk."

Lily looked up at her sister. Maggie's face had become red and blotchy, her eyes watered. Her chest rose and fell strangely. Lily wanted to reach out, to touch her. But she didn't. Her sister clutched a tiny piece of the sleeve of her baggy sweater.

"I tried to throw this thing away so many times. But she won't let me," she continued. "She doesn't eat meat, so make sure she gets protein another way. Her favorite thing to eat is eggs served sunny side up on toast. She likes to watch a Studio Ghibli movie every Sunday night after church, with popcorn. And she hates wearing shoes. She'll need to -"

"Margaret," the doctor said. "I know this is a difficult decision, but you're making the right choice. Your sister will be well taken care of. And if all goes well, we may just have her back to you and your family before Christmas. You never know."

Maggie did not look him in the eye. She simply nodded stiffly. "I understand."

"Margaret, I think we should allow Lily to get a look at her room. Then perhaps we could head back to my office and finish up the paperwork and get things settled with payments."

Lily's heart began to beat as if a woodpecker's beak slammed against her chest. Maggie was twenty-four, three years older than her. She had a steady boyfriend who would soon turn into a fiancée. Her job at the local movie theatre was good for her and paid above minimum wage. Her life was secure, concrete. There were times when Lily would sit in silence and stare at her, confused and bewildered. She was baffled by Maggie's ability to exist plainly, and Lily once had despised her for it.

"Ok, sweetheart," Maggie said, "I'm going to head out now, okay?"

Lily continued to stare. She bit down on her tongue. She wouldn't permit herself to speak.

"Come on, please. Just say something," Maggie begged, her tone harsher.

Lily refused; that power she was able to reserve for herself. She moved towards her sister, desperate for something to do to her. She was unsure if she wanted to slap her, to rest their foreheads together, or shake her and scream, 'Can you hear me? Can you see me? Do you know that I'm here?'

"I want you to listen to me, and you listen well. You signed the form yourself, you agreed to this. Don't say that you didn't. I know you want to get better, this place could be the answer," Maggie snapped.

Lily blinked and moved towards Maggie, her arms spread open awkwardly like a chick's wings. She went to encircle her sister and wrap herself around Maggie. Maggie recoiled at the contact but didn't back away. Lily's chin rested just above Maggie's shoulder strangely. The two of them didn't fit together. It was almost painful to embrace.

"I wish I wasn't," Lily whispered in her ear.

Maggie pulled back sharply and grabbed at her brown ponytail. "You never make any sense."

Maggie turned away, straightened her jacket, and moved down the hallway. The doctor looked back at Lily for a moment, then followed behind Maggie. His stride was not nearly as long as her's. Lily watched as Maggie's ponytail swished back and forth against her down coat. Their footsteps faded as they turned the corner until finally there was no sound to suggest that they were ever there. Ghosts, lost to her.

A creaking startled her. She spun in a circle. The bathroom door had partly swung open and a young woman had stepped out. Lily froze, her whole body iced down. The other girl's stare was wide-eyed and frightful, her hand rested on the handle of the bathroom door. The two of them watched one another like rabbits who could not decide if they were being hunted. Lily swallowed and made the first move as to rub her arms up and down. She ducked her head and went deeper into the room. Her bags had already been stacked neatly beside her bed, as though she had arrived at a luxury resort for the winter.

She walked across the carpeted floor to her luggage and did not meet the other girl's eye. She heard her shuffle around the room and out of the corner of her eye she watched her perch on the other bed. Their room was altogether silent, with the only sound being the prick of suppressed movement.

Lily clicked open her first bag. Neatly stacked clothing spilled out and onto the ground. Her fingers went numb with embarrassment and her throat dried. She heard squeaking and hard raps emanate from the other girl's bed. Lily looked up.

The woman held up a small whiteboard with black letters which spelled out, "Do you need any help?"

Lily's brow furrowed slightly.

"N – no. Fine, thanks."

The girl frowned. Her mouth cracked open. She spun the whiteboard around, quickly scribbled more before revealing it again. "Sorry, I'm deaf and I can't speak. I have a hard time reading lips from far away. Sorry."

Lily's hands hovered over her clothes. She glanced down for a moment and then went to sit on her bed. She began to sign, "Do you know ASL?"

The girl brightened and her whiteboard was quickly forgotten. She signed back, "Yes! It's been so long since I've met anyone who knows how to sign."

Lily could not help but grin in return. "My name is Lily," she replied in sign. "I just got here. My sister forgot to tell me that I had a roommate."

The woman smiled with the corner of her mouth. "Almost everyone has to double up. I've been here forever, and I've never had my own room. Not for very long at least. My name is Aurora."

Lily saw that she was beautiful in a celestial way. Her deep brown skin very nearly glowed, and tight spiral ringlets rested close to her head like a halo. She was ethereal, astral. There was something not quite real about her. Lily could feel it, yet she was drawn to her. She had a warmth that Lily herself did not possess.

"Nice to meet you," Lily signed cordially, not sure what else to say.

Aurora beamed. "Nice to meet you. How did you learn to sign?"

Lily cocked her head a little, as she grew uncomfortable. "I only started speaking when I was ten. Up until then, sign was all I would use."

Aurora's smile loosened. "Why?"

She took a slow breath inward. Behind Aurora's shoulder was a window, and Lily's gaze turned to the outside. Beyond the field and toward the wooded forest, she saw a hulking, shadowed figure lurking. She could not see his eyes, but she knew that he stared at her. She clenched her teeth, her body seized up. Lightning seared through her and she looked back to Aurora. She wanted to scream, 'because he wouldn't let me.'

Instead, she simply signed, "No reason."

Aurora leaned back slightly, her eyes scanned Lily up and down. Lily turned away and returned to unpacking. They allowed the room to go silent again.

***

"Welcome to group therapy. I'd like to remind everyone that this is a safe place to discuss your anxiety disorders, there is no judgment. We are all equals here. Today, we are very excited to welcome a new friend, Lily. Would you care to introduce yourself, dear?" The Doctor said. His too-wide smile cut into his cheeks.

Lily shook her head sharply. Her cheeks reddened.

"Alright, alright. That's fine. Today you can just observe, see how things run. Yes?"

She gathered her knees up to her chest. Her hair dropped around her shoulders like a cloak.

"Alright, well, uh, Amanda, would you like to start us off today?"

"Ok, sure," a female voice responded.

"Is there anything creepier than when old men call you pet-names?" someone whispered to her.

Lily looked through her hair. The man with the blue eyes and the ebony hair sat next to her. He smelled of clean linen.

He had his legs crossed. His gaze wasn't on her. "My old agent always called me 'baby', and I wanted to implode every fucking time."

Lily failed to suppress a snicker that traveled through her. She straightened up but kept her shoulders hunched. He grinned at her.

"He always thought being a pervert was some sort of a turn-on. Glad to know it's universal," he continued, his tone deadpan.

Lily's cheeks began to throb with soreness from her attempt to quell her smile. "Stop."

"If you're ever lonely, you know what to do," he said, his deep voice cracked from repressed laughter.

"Just be a creep?" she answered playfully.

"Exactly, it works," he replied.

"Poe?" The doctor said suddenly. "Poe, would you like to share with the group? How have things been going this past week?"

His smile faded, and his curly black hair fell over his forehead. "Ah, fine. Good. Haven't had any panic attacks in twelve days. It's a new record."

The group members smiled and offered him light congratulations.

The doctor put his arms up in the air. "That's fantastic, Poe. It's a great achievement. How does it make you feel?"

He cocked one eyebrow and shrugged. "Great, I guess."

The doctor leaned forward and rested his elbows on his knees. "You guess?"

Poe's eyes grew tender and he glanced downward. "I feel like I'm about to burst out sobbing every five seconds. I'm aware of myself in a way I never have been before, and I don't know what to do. The meds are helping. I know they're helping, but they're changing me, and I don't know how to feel about it."

The doctor's grin twisted into a contorted frown. "Yes. Totally understandable. It's a process. Would anyone like to respond to Poe's comments?"

A young woman with a bun nodded and began to speak back to the group. Lily looked back to Poe. All the light had drained from his face.

Lily swallowed and clenched the side of her chair while she leaned over to whisper to him, "My choreographer used to call me 'angel ass'."

Poe's eyes widened. He pursed his lips and covered his mouth.

"No. *Fuck*. 'Angel ass?' Are you fucking serious?" he whispered.

She nodded, biting her lip. She watched him as he chuckled. A flicker of sparks had lit up and warmed her body. He was exquisite. She had to fight the urge to press her arm against his and rest her head on his shoulder. Slowly, their giggling died away. They stayed quiet next to one another as the rest of the group talked.

Lily, without considering, leaned over and whispered, "I'm not crazy."

He did not look at her. "I know."

Chapter 2
The Present, Poe

Lily pretended to watch *The Wizard of Oz* on the small television in the common room. Snow sprinkled down from swirling grey clouds and littered the ground in soft white. She knew it would not be cold enough to stick. The sun would have melted it away by noon the next day. One arm was wrapped around her torso, the other combed absentmindedly through her bangs and down her thick, bone-straight blonde hair. It was heavy against her scalp and reached down to the mid-section of her back.

"So, how'd you end up here?" a low voice questioned behind her.

She jumped and flipped her gaze over her shoulder. Poe sauntered towards her, his hands in his pockets with a smirk across his face.

"I'd heard they weren't accepting anyone new. Too many crazy people, not enough beds." He plopped into the loveseat beside her.

Lily found herself suddenly relaxed. "My sister's best friend's cousin from high school works here. He did her a favor."

He smirked. "Sister's best friend's cousin. Jesus."

Lily flinched but tried to keep her smile steady. "You?"

"Oh, I used to be famous," he said. "Famous people always get top priority. And I know how this'll sound, but don't you know who I am?"

Lily shifted in her chair. "No. We don't have the internet at home."

Poe's face sobered. "God. Really? Are you Amish or something?"

"No."

"I won *American Idol* a few years back. I'm a violinist. I used to be. It feels like forever since I played. I'd probably be shit if I tried it now."

Lily replied, her voice again too high-pitched. "That's nice."

"I thought if I just got famous, if I got rich and everyone loved me, then I'd be happy. Reality TV made me rich, famous, people love me, but nothing changed. I stayed the same, the way I felt stayed the same. It's like I expected some big climax, like in a movie, but instead everything just kind of petered out. Within a year or so, most of my fans lost interest in me. I became a fallen idol if you'll pardon the term."

"That's sad."

He broke eye contact and looked at the carpet. "The only thing that made me feel good was alcohol. When I started drinking, I couldn't stop. I was ruining my body, driving everyone away, humiliating myself in public. I didn't have a choice but to do something, anything." He paused, then cleared his throat. "The Doctor tells me it's a coping mechanism."

For a moment, Lily despised him. Everything he did he did to himself. He'd obtained more success at his young age than most people would in a lifetime. She'd gladly trade her defective mind for his. She wanted him to see what it was like to live in a collapsing star, constantly imploding. She wished he could understand the pain, the fire. He was ungrateful. Ungrateful. She laced her fingers together to keep them from flying into his face and ripping his eye from its socket.

"Oh," she said.

He leaned back into his seat. He was truly skinny and looked unhealthy.

"I want to get better though, you know? Really," he said. "I want to get better for my boyfriend at least. When I decided to come here, it was like we both felt hope for the first time in a while. It felt like I could breathe. Maybe that's unhealthy in itself. But I can't go back, I can't be with him again until I'm better. He deserves so much more than just me."

She saw that his eyes had reddened and watered. He ducked his head so his curls covered them.

"How long has it been since the two of you spoke?" She was suddenly desperate to touch him.

He curled his body up into a ball. "Three months or so. He said that he needed time."

"Have you written to him? Maybe that's a good start." In truth, she had no idea what a 'good start' would entail.

"I've tried. He knows where I am. He could always visit. I just don't think he's ready yet."

Lily bit the scabs on her lips. "What's his name?"

When he finally looked up, she saw that his eyes were dazed, as if he'd been sedated and tranquilized. "Shepherd," he said.

She had never seen anyone so clearly ravished by love. He had allowed himself to be dominated by it. He had given something in his soul to this man, with no guarantee that their futures would align.

She knew him. She recognized him. She felt a tingling below her waist and prickling in her breast. She hunched down, embarrassed by the primitive reactions of her body.

"Lily," The Doctor's voice summoned her.

Something about his voice parched her spirit. She turned around in her chair to watch him as he approached her.

"I have some very exciting news. Your equestrian volunteer is here."

She looked out the window. "It's snowing."

The Doctor laughed. "I don't think that'll be a problem. This girl is from the mountains, so are her horses. The cold doesn't bother them."

"What about me?"

"If you'd rather not go out, I can tell her to come back in a few days."

Stress made the moths flutter more furiously throughout her brain. Their wings slapped against the inside of her skull. She sighed loudly, irritated by her actions and the actions of The Doctor.

"No, it's fine," she said. "I'll get my scarf and gloves."

"Good, good, dear." He laid his hand across her shoulder.

Fire. Fire on her skin.

"Do not touch me," she roared.

Everyone in the common room turned to look at her. The air was still and silent. It echoed only with her panting breath. Even Poe looked frightened of her. She allowed her hair to fall over her in a shield. She rushed away and off towards her room.

When she got to her room, the moths quieted, exhaustion calmed their wings. She paused in the doorway. Aurora lay on her bed reading *War and Peace* by Tolstoy.

She glanced up. "Hello."

The moths settled and landed on the soft plush of her gray brain at the sight of Aurora, their wings smoothed to a gentle beating rap as they rested. Lily brought her hands up to her ears, her fingernails clenched in her scalp.

"So stupid, so stupid, so stupid," she scolded herself.

"What happened?" Aurora signed.

"Nothing. I always act like such an idiot. Everything makes me so angry and I lose my temper. I'm so stupid. I'm so stupid."

"No," she signed back. "No. Don't call yourself 'stupid.' I hate that word. You aren't stupid."

Shame flooded Lily and made her chest icy. She fetched her red scarf from the desk and slipped on her gloves. She searched for an excuse to change the subject and gestured to Aurora's copy of *War and Peace*.

"I read that my senior year of high school," she signed. "Pierre is my favorite."

Aurora rested her body back against the pillows. "I've always wanted to finish it. I always give up. Not this time."

Lily found herself smiling while her stomach warmed. She watched Aurora for a few moments and took in her face. She felt, somehow, as though she had been looking for this girl and had not realized it until that very moment. She nibbled at her lip and jutted her chin downward before turning away. She wrapped her scarf around her neck, going out through the hall and toward the main entrance. She did not say goodbye. She continued until she saw a misty figure stand outside.

The receptionist cleared her throat and Lily turned to look at her. Her lips dipped into a nervous frown.

The receptionist smiled and asked softly, "Lily?"

Lily nodded.

The receptionist pointed to the blurred figure outside. "She's waiting for you. Stay warm out there and have a fabulous time."

Lily felt a chill travel through her arms and legs. She looked forward and headed outside before the receptionist could say anything more. The cold hit her hard. The being who stood before her was turned away. All Lily could see were bundles of russet corkscrew curls that traveled down her back.

"Sorry? I'm Lily. I think you're waiting for me?"

The girl turned around. A blazing flash of light shot through Lily's mind. A vision glittered before her, sparkling and brilliant. It was a vividness she'd never known. A memory burst through her brain with illuminated flashes of color and light; she almost recoiled from the force of it. The vision she saw was of a mounted stag's head, bolted up to a cream-colored wall. The air hung thick around the murdered stag's decapitated head. Its cold, black marble eyes stared into the deepest pools of her soul. Its antlers were frozen in time, caught in an inescapable purgatory.

Lily staggered backward. She threw her arms out as she attempted to steady herself.

The girl reached out and grabbed hold of her elbow. "Woah, woah, woah. You okay?"

Lily's hands flew over the other woman's knuckles.

"Sorry, sorry. Dizzy. I get dizzy spells." She lied.

She opened her eyes and for the first time, she saw the woman clearly.

She had a full figure, natural and curvy, with defined muscles visible across her sculpted arms. Her skin was a dark olive, smooth, and silken. Her curls were twisted in tight, frizzy ringlets. The winter air blew through them freely.

"Do I need to get a doctor? Do you need me to call someone?"

Lily burst out of her trance and looked down at the woman's grip, which was still locked onto her elbow. "No, no. No, I'm sorry. I'm sorry."

"Right," she said tentatively. "Okay."

Lily swallowed a painful lump of saliva, it traveled down her throat like a hunk of coal. "I'm sorry, I don't ... I don't know your name."

"Right. I'm Seraphina. Seraphina Ramsey. You knew I was coming, yeah?"

Lily's gaze flickered between Seraphina's lips and eyes. "Yeah."

Seraphina scanned Lily. "You know you're supposed to go riding with me today?"

Lily allowed a tight breath of air trapped in her throat to escape slowly through her nostrils. "Yes."

"Do you feel alright to ride?"

"I'm fine, really," Lily replied. Her voice was deeper than usual.

"If you say so. But if I see the tiniest wobble while you're in that saddle, I'm pulling you down. Understood?"

Lily cleared her throat, "Okay."

Seraphina sighed before snickering softly under her breath. "Aren't you freezing?"

"No, not really," Lily lied. She glanced over Seraphina's thin jacket and faded jeans, meeting her worn-down riding boots at the calf. "Aren't you?"

"I was born in the mountains. I haven't felt cold in years."

Seraphina showed her gums when she smiled. She glanced back over her shoulder. "I tied the horses up over there. Follow me, yeah?"

She began to walk forward without another word and Lily floated behind, within her shadow.

"What experience do you have with horses?" Seraphina said.

"I grew up on a farm."

"That doesn't answer my question."

Lily's steps faltered. "I rode all the time when I was little. I guess I stopped about, um, ten or so years ago."

"Better than nothing. Why did you quit?"

"It started to feel wrong."

"What does that mean?"

"I don't know."

"No," Seraphina said. "You said it, I just want to know what you meant."

Lily stared down at the snow caked to her shoes. "I felt weird. It started to seem like the horses were smarter than me, like they understood something I couldn't. It felt wrong, they were supposed to be running free and wild on some plain, not trotting in circles to entertain me."

Seraphina's stiff, marble expression cracked into a slight grin. "I see."

"It's a personal thing. I didn't mean that you…"

"No, no. I think it's sweet. You're sweet."

Lily tried to reply, but only a low gurgle emerged.

They rounded a tree and approached two large mares secured to the trunk. Seraphina stroked the stockier one's neck.

"This one's Pharaoh. Isn't she stunning? The other one is yours, her name's Pixie."

Pixie was taller than Pharaoh. Whereas Pharaoh was sharp obsidian, contrasting vividly with the white of the snow, Pixie's coat was colored a soft cotton, speckled with coal-black spots. Lily stood to Pixie's side, frozen as she watched the animal puff out clouds from her nostrils.

"Come on," Seraphina said. "I chose Pixie for you because she's so gentle. I doubt she'd buck you even if a rat ran up her leg. I brought some riding boots for you too. I was told you wear a size six. I hope you'll be able to wear my sevens because that's all I've got. Here, hold onto my shoulder."

Lily did as she commanded. Her frozen shoes slipped away from her feet, replaced by thick boots.

"There we go, do those feel alright?"

Lily did not answer. She did not allow herself to break Pixie's gaze. She found herself stepping forward. Her fingers extended toward the mare. Before she could consider it, her fingertips brushed up against Pixie's mane. Pixie blinked. Her gaze flickered over Lily. Lily's lower lip quivered.

"Forgive me?" she whispered to the mare.

"What's that?" Seraphina asked.

Lily's tongue grazed over her lips as she cleared her throat. "Nothing."

"Do you need help getting in the saddle? Or do you remember how to do it yourself?"

Lily glanced at Seraphina. "Yes, I remember."

She hoisted herself up onto the horse. Her feet slid into the stirrup. She looked down at Seraphina, who appeared slightly impressed. Seraphina rose onto her own horse as well, doing so with far more grace and elegance than Lily had.

Seraphina offered guidance to Lily when it came to her command of Pixie, yet her words flew past Lily's ears.

Lily's head bobbed to the side while she watched Seraphina's curls sway back and forth across the back of her jacket. She listened to the music of her voice, even and melodic.

Lily had never known any significant desire for touch. She despised the sensation of flesh against her flesh. Yet as she looked at Seraphina, she wondered how her breasts would feel cupped within her hands. She wondered how her torso and hips curved when her clothes slid off of them.

"Lily?"

"Sorry, what?"

"I asked where you were from. It clearly isn't here."

"I'm from a little town down in the valley. I haven't been to the mountains since I was little."

"And did anything exciting ever happen in your town in the valley?"

"My graduating class was forty-six people."

Seraphina laughed. "I'll take that as a 'no.' I never went to any public school myself, my mother taught me everything I know. She didn't make me memorize any bullshit lies about the history of America and what a hero Christopher Columbus was. She made me understand how things are. She taught me how the Earth and how everything in it is all part of one spirit. She made me realize how beautiful and fragile life really is. She taught me that we are all connected, that our existence is rare and precious. I learned more from her than anyone of those forty-six people you graduated with."

"That's probably true. I don't really remember much from high school. I don't remember the books we read or the facts we had to memorize for our tests. It's all kind of a blur, really'"

"I wish you were from the mountains. You'd have loved my mother. She'd have loved you, too. And I think the two of us could have been friends, don't you?"

"I've never had many friends."

Why had she said that?

"Neither did I. The other kids always thought I was weird, they never wanted to play with me. It seems silly, but I look back on it and it makes me sad."

Lily's shoulders tightened. "Sometimes I think the worst thing ever is loneliness."

Seraphina was silent for many moments before she twisted around to look at Lily. "That's true, isn't it?"

"Maybe."

Seraphina's eyes softened. "We don't have to talk if you don't want to. We can just ride. Let's just ride for a little while."

Lily felt a tear travel down her cheek. She lifted her hand to slap it away shamefully, nodding in brisk cuts. "That'd be nice, I think."

"We never have to make small talk. We can just hang out together. I'm doing this for you, remember. I want to help you. If that means that one week we don't say a single word to each other, then that's okay. Boring people are the ones who need to talk all the time."

"You don't think I'm boring?"

Seraphina smiled openly, with her teeth and gums, and turned away again. "No, sweetheart, I don't."

Lily nibbled at her lower lip as warmth blossomed in her chest to replace the cold of winter.

***

Lily's limbs relaxed on the arms of the small sofa. Her fingers throbbed with the craving to run through Seraphina's curls. She imagined the sway of her hips, the dipping of her ringlets down her back. She picked away at the bloody crater on her lower lip with her teeth.

The door opened and The Doctor stepped into the room.

"So sorry to be late, dear. So, so sorry. The nurse shouldn't have left you in my office alone, it won't happen again. I swear."

The Doctor dropped down onto his chair directly in front of her.

"So," he began. "How are things going so far? I saw you with Poe, that's a great step in your process. It's always a positive thing to make friends."

The Doctor's office was ominous, foreboding. It held the sensation of freezing to death. It chilled the body before numbing it. It fooled the body into submission by promising to give it the sensation of warmth. The body is dead before it realizes that it's all a trick.

"You seemed comfortable with Poe. Do you feel comfortable talking with me?"

Lily shrugged.

"How did things go with Seraphina?"

A smile pushed itself onto her lips. "Good."

The Doctor's shoulders straightened. He slapped his thighs. "Well, that's fantastic. Do you think you'd like to continue with the program?"

"Yes," she answered softly.

"That's great news, wonderful news. Wonderful. And have you heard from your sister at all since arriving at Meadowlark?"

"No."

He nodded. "How do you feel about that? Are you happy to have a break? Or are you feeling lonely?"

She clenched her toes. "I don't know."

"You have always lived at home, is that correct?"

"Yes."

"Do you ever feel as if she is stifling you? Perhaps as though she is trying to control you?"

Her fingers fisted into her sweatpants. "I don't want to talk about Maggie."

The Doctor pushed his back into the seat. "Alright. Did the nurse make it clear what will happen this session?"

"Therapy."

"Yes, well, yes. Here at Meadowlark Farm, we like to approach the healing process holistically. The mind works in strange ways, psychotherapy and medications are wonderful, but they are merely individual tools in a much larger tool chest. If we expand our thinking, who knows what else we can find?"

She stared at him, unblinking. He was not human. He couldn't be.

"Okay," she responded.

"How do you feel about hypnosis?"

"What?"

The Doctor held up his hands. "Give it a chance before you say 'no'. Now, hypnosis has many negative connotations because of television and Hollywood. But it is really a misunderstood art. It is a process, of course. But I have been practicing hypnotherapy for many years now, I'm a trained professional. You can trust me."

She imagined that he was a wind-up toy that could only be activated when a key was spun within his back. Someone invisible was always there to twist the key and allow him to speak.

"I do need your consent. If you really do not wish to take part in this, I will understand. You must *want* it to work."

"Okay. Fine. Yes," she replied. Why had she said that?

"Marvelous. Marvelous. Then, let us begin. We shall take it easy today."

He scooted his chair closer to her. "Now, hypnotherapy works best after being performed multiple times. The first session typically will not yield the most fruitful results, so, please be patient."

She nodded.

"I want you to relax. Let go. Let go. Let go. And you're gone."

Chapter 3
The Past, Supernova

I leaned over the toilet as bile ran down my throat and into the bowl. I spit out the last of the vomit. Once I finished, I straightened my crown and feathered headdress.

"Lily? Is everything okay?" A voice called from the other side of the restroom door.

I looked sharply to the side. My quivering hands fell to my hips. "Yes. Sorry, I'm just getting ready. How much time?"

"Fifteen until curtain."

Illness rose in my stomach again and I lunged for the porcelain bowl. My head spun and my legs felt weak. "I'll be out soon."

"Are you sure you're alright?" The voice asked again. It might have been Cynthia.

"Yes," I snapped. "I'll be out soon."

I knew that she hadn't gone because I heard shuffling and whispering. I gripped the toilet lid and lowered myself to the floor, rocking back and forth on my calves. The grungy beige tile chilled my legs through the tights. I pulled my feet with my pointe shoes attached out from underneath me as I leaned back against the bathroom wall.

"Lily? Can you hear me?" A different voice called. I recognized it right away as Colton. My heart began to pound and my throat dried again.

"Yeah, I can."

"Do you need help? Do you want me to get Charmaine?"

I shook my head, even though I knew he couldn't see.

"No. I'm fine, thank you," I said, my voice too high-pitched to be authentic.

He was quiet for a moment, then said, "Are you nervous? Because, like, there's no reason to be. You've been so crazy good in rehearsal."

I bit down on my lip and locked my hands on my hips. I rose from my position on the floor, my gaze locked on my shoes as I went toward the bathroom mirror. I looked at myself.

"You're going to be so wonderful tonight, I know it," Colton said. "You've worked so hard for this. This is your night."

I could not break my focus from my reflection. My costume and the feathers on my headdress were a deep cardinal red. My crown and bodice were decorated with fake diamonds and rose-colored jewels, concentrated around the torso and breasts, accented with gold. My skirt was thick, yet loose and flowing, cut into sheer plume-like strips. My tiara had a false ruby that dipped into my forehead. My feathered headdress was fluffed. It rose high and plunged down my neck. My hair was bundled up, wrapped into a braided bun. My eyeliner was bulky, my eyeshadow was the color of flaming crimson and wine; the wings flared out onto my cheekbones.

For the first time in my life, I was beautiful. My breath caught in my throat and my fingertips moved to rest against the mirror. Even my ugly upturned nose looked lovely and highlighted. My freckles were covered, and my dark, clunky eyebrows were blended. My waist was cinched. My nails were manicured.

I was beautiful.

I had always despised the flabby skin on my stomach and my short, thin nails. I hated my unplucked eyebrows and the thickness of my thighs. I hated my bunions and curve of the arches of my feet. I hated my pointed nose. I hated my blotchy skin and freckles. I hated my hair.

"We're ten minutes until curtain, Lil'," Colton said. "You know, once you get on stage, something happens. You transform. You were meant to be the Firebird. You're going to blow the crowd away."

Colton was playing Prince Ivan. I thought back to our rehearsals; just the two of us together in the studio. I remembered the pressure of his fingers around my waist, the warmth in his eyes as he watched me move. I looked toward the door, moving to where his voice emanated from. In truth, I could hardly recall the last time he spoke my name. The moths eating my brain away began to quiet, the fluttering of their wings faded as they landed on my skull.

I wished I could tell him what I knew. I wished he knew that my right ankle was weak and that my left Achilles tendon was ruined. I did not know how to say that I had heard a pop in our last rehearsal, a tiny explosion somewhere. I did not know how to say that the pain in my back was agony. I did not know how to admit to him that every step was torture. I did not know how to say that I was nineteen and that my body was decaying. I wanted to run out on stage and scream that I was dying. I looked at myself in the mirror again.

I was beautiful for the first and last time. I bent down and washed out my mouth with frigid water from the sink. When I pushed myself upright again, my head swam and burned. Lava was trapped inside, the pressure ached. I moved slowly toward the bathroom door and pressed it open. Outside, I saw Colton and a small group of women from the corps. Their faces brightened when they saw me emerge. I would have died for them then. Colton was dressed fully in his black tights and bejeweled vest along with his white shirt. My heart lurched as he smiled at me.

"Lily, you look so pretty." He offered me his arm.

The other girls crowded around me. They wished me luck and touched me. I did not want to push them away. I wanted to press myself against their skins until we'd melded together. They did not know that I was losing a race. They couldn't see that I was falling behind. Our success had to be unified, joint. I was the collective. We were the collective.

"Five minutes, Colton," a stagehand said.

Colton was calm. Colton was absolutely serene. This would not be the end for him. This would be the beginning of a glorious future. He let me go once he was sure that I would cooperate.

He went to the prop counter and picked up his bow and arrow. He turned back to me. His oblong face was so soft.

"Leave everything out on that stage tonight. I know you can do it."

Everything in me ached to touch him.

The orchestra had already begun the overture. Colton smiled at me once more, then held his arms out and entered stage right.

It was Stravinsky Night at the Pink Ribbon Theater. We had just finished a performance of *Petrushka* and a shortened version of *The Rite of Spring*, neither of which I was a part of. My choreographer said he wanted to conserve me. I did not tell him that I had scheduled surgery for the upcoming week. My first season as a company member would be my last. I knew that I needed to supernova. I needed to let them watch me implode in on myself.

I felt cool fingertips against my bare shoulders. I jumped back. Cynthia stared at me. She was playing the principal princess, but I knew she wanted the Firebird. The sharp, passive hatred in her eyes told me as much. That same hatred once fueled me. The way I could excel, my talent, my obsession, it had sparked jealousy in my peers that electrified me. Yet, as I watched Cynthia stare at me, her eyes bright with resentment, I felt nothing.

"Good luck out here, sweetie," she told me. "You're going to kill it."

My music cue made my ears prick up. Adrenaline burned my chest as I faced forward. With a single leap, I was on stage. And that was that.

I no longer existed outside of the bounds of the audience. The blinding light of the stage extinguished me as clapping enfolded my ears, drowning me. I began my zestful variation, playfully bounding up on my pointe shoes and whirling around the stage. I relished my freedom, but Colton lurked behind a set-piece, waiting to entrap me. I wondered if he could see that I was already beginning to sweat, or that I wanted to cry out for the pain in my feet, legs, and back. Every moment was fire.

Colton's arms circled loosely around my torso. I fought against him, careful to remember my blocking. A rush of panic seeped through me. He held me tighter than usual. I cast my eyes down and saw that he had laced his fingers together. My lips parted and my breathing became staggered and uneven. I wanted to turn around and push him back, but I knew I could not. I flapped my arms and forced myself to remain graceful and balanced.

Fire poured into the marrow of my bones. I was willing to tear Prince Ivan apart to release myself from his cage. I was willing to end him and myself if necessary. I grunted slightly, twisting myself away from him. He lifted me up, and I flew. I angled my head upward, soaking in the warmth from the stage lights. I beat my wings as I was lowered back down to the ground. He took hold of my hand as he spun me, and I did whatever possible to break away from him.

My choreographer had not been satisfied with the original plot of *The Firebird*. It had not made sense to him that the Firebird should beg for her life from the prince. Why should something so mystical and otherworldly be subservient to a mortal? I spun and danced around Ivan wildly. He leaped to the other side of the stage. We moved in sync, but my power quickly overtook his. He was foolish to venture into the woods at all. My woods. And all at once, we froze. An agreement was struck between us. He understood that I was not meant to be taken prisoner, and I respect that he learned a lesson. I plucked a feather from my headdress and handed it to him. If he should ever find himself in dire straits, I could be summoned. There is a bond between us now.

I was five when I began to dance. After I was exiled from my Catholic preschool for biting the other children so hard that blood was drawn, my parents were desperate to find an outlet for me. I excelled quickly and was placed in an advanced class the next year.

Prince Ivan called for me when he was surrounded by the monstrous creatures of the forest. He was afraid and he needed me. I materialized, and everything in the forest is enraptured by me. I made them dance the Infernal Dance, I forced them to continue until madness or exhaustion overtook them. One by one, each of the beings collapsed. The forest was hushed, and I smoothed my feathers. Prince Ivan's eyes watered.

My parents had not known that I was too young to be dancing at the level that I was; my teachers had convinced them that my early talent was valuable, so valuable that the intensive training was justified. I can hardly remember a time when I was not engaged in a rehearsal or busied preparing for a role. My lack of friends and social life were excused by my parents in my search for perfection. At ten, I starred in *The Nutcracker* as Clara. After the performance, I said, "My feet hurt." They were the first words I spoke. The look of betrayal on my parent's face was etched in my memory. I was forbidden to sign in the house again.

Ivan had fallen in love with the most ravishing of the thirteen princesses who resided in the forest as captives of Koschei the Immortal. I could still remember the light and warmth which existed in my lands before Koshei invaded. Koschei had kept my forest under his rule for too long. I had tried to ignore it. This was the time. I knew the opportunity would not arise again. I had allowed him to take over, but his reign was at an end. I would grant the princesses and Ivan their freedom, just as the prince granted me mine.

I was fifteen when my body began to give signs of spoiling. I was performing the Danse des Petits Cygnes in the Pink Ribbon's production of *Swan Lake* when I discovered what pain meant. I was dancing as the furthest swan on the left; the stage lighting was a deeply saturated blue that bathed all of us in its glow. The desperation to remain synchronized with the other girls was almost paralyzing, and my chest felt as though it was about to burst. As we worked to finish the *pas de quatre*, I felt a snap in my left Achilles Tendon. Pain shot up through my leg and into my stomach as if lightning had struck me. My breath halted and my lips drifted open. I almost whimpered, and all that I could see was a blue spotlight. I rode to the hospital in my pancake tutu.

Ivan defeated the evil wizard Koshei, but destroyed his immorality in the process. The duel was a formidable one. With Ivan's victory, the forest was set free. The princesses were finally out of his grasp, and I knew that Ivan understood what this would mean. The kingdoms and the forest would enter a new era. I would have my power over the woods again.

I never fully recovered from the ruination of my left Achilles tendon, and the injuries quickly grew in multitude and severity. Physical therapy and surgeries became standard, yet I continued to plummet. For the second time, I danced in *The Nutcracker* as a snowflake and the Dew-Drop Fairy, understudying for the Sugar Plum Fairy, though I never got to perform the part. With every moment, I was in excruciating pain. Every doctor I saw made it clear that my body was not made for the art form. Yet, as I danced as the snowflake, false white powder dropped onto our hair from the rafters, I floated. The Beast did not have a hold of me. I was free. And when I danced the Waltz of the Flowers as the Dew-Drop Fairy, the stage lights were dimmed. I saw the faces of the audience as they were enchanted by me. I made them feel something other than fear or pain or hatred. Whoever I was offstage did not have to exist. Still, no matter my efforts, there was not a doctor who could heal me, my body was already too broken. Too late.

Ivan and the princess wedded. The other women attended as honored guests. The music grew, building as we reached the finale. The audience could not see me yet, but I was there. I watched from an elevated platform as the celebration moved to its climax. My eyes misted over. My throat clenched. They were free because of me. The spotlight fell on me and my shadow was projected in mammoth proportion. Ivan and the princesses got on their knees, their hands and arms raised to me. The crowd began to clap spiritedly, as if their hands could not come together fast enough. I am up on pointe with my feet together in a *relevé,* I was beating my wings. I was consumed as the curtain fell and the audience was left spellbound.

I, supernova.

Chapter 4
The Present, Soap

"Okay, Lily, come back. Come back. Come back," The Doctor said. "You're awake now. You're awake."

Lily lifted the back of her quaking hand to wipe the sweat away from her upper lip. "I don't feel well."

"Yes. I'm sorry, dear. I've never had a first session bring up those kinds of memories and emotions. Are you alright?"

She panted as her gaze slowly lifted to look The Doctor in the face. "I died that night. I died on that stage."

"You did not die, dear."

"Did Maggie tell you I tried to kill myself after the performance?"

"She did."

"I went into my mother's bathroom and swallowed a full bottle of her sleeping pills, then I drank half of Grey Goose my parents kept locked in the cabinet. It tasted horrible, it almost made me throw-up. It made my stomach and throat burn. My mother was angry because she wouldn't be able to refill the prescription on her sleeping pills for another month, and my father made me pay him back for the vodka."

The Doctor barely moved. "And how did you..."

"Maggie caught me and made me go to the hospital. They pumped my stomach."

"Why did you do it?"

38

"Because I was dead already. I was a cold, ugly, walking corpse. My life ended when the performance did." Lily replied, her throat clenched and dry.

"Why do you feel that way?"

"I knew my career was over. I'd never dance again, not really."

"But why does the end of your dancing mean the end of your life?"

Her chest ached. Her left arm went numb.

"I've got to go back to my room."

"I'm not sure that that's a good idea."

"Fuck you," she hissed.

He frowned deeply. "What?"

"Fuck you," she screamed. "Fuck you."

She bounded up, yanked a large print of Van Gogh's *Bedroom in Arles* off the wall. She hurled it across the room. It slammed into the desk, only just missed The Doctor. He jumped up from his chair, as it sailed out of the way.

"I want to go to my room," she shrieked. Her thundering voice reverberated off the wall.

Her bellows rippled across the space between them, making her ears ring as the painting lay bent and mutilated in the corner. The Doctor pushed his fingers through his balding, gelled hair. Lily's eyes fell to the window. She saw the Beast's colossal form stalk the two of them, watching. Watching. She had pleased him. His cool blue eyes bored into hers. Her spirit grew tranquil, and her lips parted as she realized what she'd done. She blinked to see past the tears, desperate to find a way to apologize. The words refused to fly from her lips. They simply remained fixed to the inside of her mouth and blistered her tongue like puss-filled sores. Guilt twisted through her insides.

"Can I go to my room now?" she asked.

She wanted to mend the painting herself with her bone and muscle, to pull the blood out of her veins to fix the frame.

The Doctor did not look at her. "I will send Nurse Cathy to make sure everything is alright in a few minutes."

Her eyes continued to mist and her lip quivered, but she left the room before he could see.

***

Lily pretended to watch *The Wizard of Oz* in the common room. Snow fluttered down from the silver sky. She could almost feel the cold from her position.

"I wonder why they think a man screaming in a lion fur suit is the peak of cinema. They play this on loop, but I can't pretend that Judy Garland doesn't make up for it, at least a little," Poe said.

She could not muster the energy to turn and acknowledge him.

"I'm almost positive that the definition of insanity is trying the same thing over and over that doesn't succeed, and knowing all the time. I feel like we've entered *The Twilight Zone*," he said, his legs flung over the arm of the chair directly beside Lily's.

She did not meet his smile. "Uh-huh."

"What's wrong?" he finally asked. "Hard session?"

She nodded.

He sighed, loudly and deeply. "Ah."

She wanted to twist his ebony hair within her fingers and rip it out from the root, leaving his scalp sore and bloody. "I'm always tired."

She was unsure why she had said that. She wished she hadn't.

"How old are you?" he asked.

She woke up a little. "Why?"

"I'm twenty-three. I'll be twenty-four in two months."

"Twenty-one." She felt so much older and so much younger concurrently.

"You go to university?"

"No. I'm a dancer. I joined a company back home right out of high school."

He rested his temple and cheek against his closed fist. "I never went to university, either. Can you guess where I'm from?"

He did have a strange accent. "I don't know. Somewhere in the UK?"

His face brightened, clearly impressed. "Good. The Scottish Highlands."

"You don't sound very Scottish."

"The price of the American Dream. I moved to the Bayou in Louisiana as a child so my father could deal heroin laced with Fentanyl more freely."

She sat up straighter.

He looked up, his bright eyes fixing to hers. "He wasn't a bad man, I don't think. He had an addiction, it turned him into something else. Have you ever been addicted to something?"

"No."

"I know it's hard to understand, easier to judge."

She shifted in her chair, her body cramping up as the words crawled out from her throat and onto her tongue, "I've had habits ... but ..."

"Really?" he asked, surprised. "What kind of habits?"

She shook her head. Her hair fell over her face. "Nothing. It's stupid."

"No, no. Tell me." He leaned forward to rest his elbows against his thighs.

She rolled her eyes, shrugged, and hid her quivering hands. "It's ridiculous. So stupid. When I was thirteen there was a fight with another girl, and I got in trouble for it. I was upset when I got home, my parents made me wash the dishes as a punishment. I was by myself. While I was pumping dish soap onto the sponge ... I don't know ... it looked like it would taste good."

Poe's face contorted. "What?"

Lily let out a frantic, breathy laugh and began to sweat.

"I told you, stupid. I just, I don't know, I took a clean glass and started to wash it. I filled it up with water, and the soap was all foamy and smelled like pearls. I don't know why I started drinking it."

He was silent.

She pinched the center of the front of her sweater with her middle finger and thumb, pulling it away from her.

"It was stupid, stupid. It tasted disgusting, but I kept drinking. I did it over and over until my stomach started cramping. I was doubled over it hurt so bad. I was acting like such a drama queen. My sister finally forced my parents to drive me to the hospital. I never told them what I did. I tried it again the next week, went to the hospital a second time. They couldn't figure out what was wrong with me. Isn't that ridiculous?" She kept up her hysterical giggling.

"Shit," Poe said. "Why didn't you tell anybody?"

"I don't know. I was embarrassed, I knew my family would make me stop. I didn't want to stop, I enjoyed it. It made me feel good. It made me feel clean. And the pain made me feel, I don't know, centered. I would wait as long as I could before I did it again. The doctors were so confused." She looked up at him, throwing her head back as if she were telling a joke.

"How long did this go on?"

"Three years or so. I didn't make myself stop until I was sixteen. I don't know why I stopped. I miss it, to be honest. My parents still don't know, neither does my sister. They think that my stomach just cleared up on its own like it was some sort of miracle. I was never sure why I was doing it anyway. It felt like all that rot and dead stuff in me was cleared away afterwards. It felt like a garden was growing in my stomach, like the pain was plants and flowers sprouting up through my intestines; like my bones could be washed."

Cottony exhaustion clotted her ears and brain in wadded balls. She realized what she'd admitted. She wanted to collapse in on herself. Supernova.

Poe looked down at his hands.

"It's just a joke. I was a stupid kid."

"I tried China White for the first time while I was with my dad," Poe said. "It was right before he overdosed. I remember throwing up and passing out, and when I woke up my dad was standing over me, laughing. He was so hideous by the time he died, his face was all mangled and he didn't weigh much more than 120 pounds. But in every picture I see from when he was young, he looked just like me."

"How old were you?"

"Thirteen or so, I think I'd just had my birthday. He thought I'd handle it better than I did."

She stared at him for a moment, then her gaze turned upward to the television. Dorothy was woefully committing to her fate as the Witch's prisoner. Little did she know how soon she would be rescued.

"I'm tired. It feels like I've been here forever."

"Lily," Poe said.

Her bones seemed to melt into pools of marrow that dripped against her muscles and nerves at the sound of his voice.

"You've got to try to take it slowly," he continued. "One day at a time. You'll go mad if you don't."

She did not answer right away, she could not even look down at him from the television set. "Isn't it crazy how quickly you can disappear? Like, quickly you can vanish and just … not exist anymore." Her gaze snapped towards him suddenly. "Never mind. Sorry."

All of the words had thawed and then evaporated from the place deep inside her throat and chest. Her lips sealed shut and her mouth was sore. She never wanted to speak again.

"It's snowing," Poe said. "I miss the cold in Scotland sometimes. It was a different kind of cold. Deep, gray clouds and wind. It felt like fucking icicles could grow in your chest, but there was something comfortable about it. Does that make any sense?"

She did not reply.

Chapter 5
The Past, December 3rd

It was December third, and I was going to kill myself. It would not be my first time to try, hardly my first. The winters were cold living at the feet of mountains. Snow could pack you in and bury you above ground until you suffocate. They would find you in summer, your fingers and nails bloodied from scratching and trying to breakthrough. They would mistake your screams for the cries of mountain lions.

The first time I heard a mountain lion scream I was six. I was out camping with my scout troop, sharing a tent with a young girl who thought she was my friend. She thought she was until I slammed her up against a wall and bit her face, then she realized she wasn't. But that had not happened yet. We were cocooned in sleeping bags but both of us were awake.

I was staring up at the tarp ceiling, my arms crossed over my chest and my plush unicorn resting on my chest. It was then that we heard a shriek that echoed through the camp, like an old god crying out. I still remember lying there, my body icebound with terror. The girl who thought she was my friend began to cry. Everyone always did say that the forest was haunted. I would never hear a mountain lion scream again. I would never do so many things ever again.

I stared at my naked body in the mirror. My hair covered most of my flat breasts and nipples, both of which were different sizes. I had gained weight in my hips since I had stopped dancing. I used to be shaped like a twig, now I more closely resembled a pear. I rose my hand to smooth down my heavy brown eyebrows. I thought for a moment that perhaps I should have plucked them, but I knew that they would do that before the funeral. I could not help but imagine myself in an open casket. I hoped that they would put me in red, it's the only color I had ever looked decent in.

A mist began to fog over the mirror as the bath filled. My reflection was lost to me from the thickness of the steam. Even with the heat already generated from the smoking bath, I felt cold and clammy. I was a corpse already. My head began to spin as I looked down at the tub while the water rose.

In the past month, the only thing I had been able to fantasize about was wearing a long, flowing dress and stepping into a lily pond, and plunging myself underneath the surface. I imagined the water would ripple above my head and block out the sun. I imagined that my body would float like I was levitating on the moon. My breath echoed in and out of my chest, and I moved to grasp the four-way cross circular medallion which hung around my neck.

"Jesus, Jesus, Jesus," I said.

I could not tell if I was crying out for Him or simply calling His name for something to say. I could not even imagine that He was listening to me. I would not have blamed Him. My family would never forgive me once they realized what I had done. If I was lucky, they considered me trapped in Purgatory, but at the funeral, they would mingle in whispers of where I truly am.

I had always imagined Hell as a place of chains and fire that would scold my skin and pierce my flesh. I looked down and my hair curtained over my face. Fear chilled my body and quickly transformed into terror. I began to squirm, my skeleton felt as though it was about to burst through my skin. I looked toward the ceiling, rose on my toes. My feet ached constantly.

"Can you see me?" It sounded as though I was begging. "Please, please, please."

I began to panic. My medallion became laced with sweat as I clutched it in my palm. All I wanted was to feel Him one last time, to feel that golden light that used to fill me to my brim. He knew that this was the end. Did He hate me so much that he would not even say goodbye?

I looked down and realized that the tub was filled, soon it would overflow. I reached over to switch off the water. Without taking the chance to consider, I plunged my feet into the scalding bath. I gritted my teeth, my throat closed as pain shot up my legs. I forced myself to bend down and dipped my full body into the boiling liquid. It was not quite hot enough to leave burns. Perspiration broke out on my forehead. My cross fell into the water. I knew that it would rust. My mother would never have spent money on real silver. There was a misted-over window directly to my right, and I saw his form outside. I sunk deeper into the tub.

The first time I saw the Beast I was still in preschool. From what my parents tell me, I wasn't any trouble before I started interacting with other children. I was an easy baby, a little early, but I rarely cried. I never screamed or threw tantrums. I was docile, like a doll who ate and drank. I was the calmest and happiest at church, which my parents took as a sign that I was blessed by the Heavens, possibly even touched by the Trinity themselves. My sister loved holding me, nearly every picture in our family scrapbooks is of me in her arms, of her sticking a bottle between my lips.

When I entered the Guardian Angels Preschool for Catholic Children, it was as though I was awakened, or at least as though the monster was. I became a terror. Every day at least five other children would leave the school with a circular bite mark on their cheeks or arms, sometimes even their necks. My father always told me 'you could drive a nun to drink.' I was expelled from the school by those same nuns my father promised that I would drive to liquor. They gave the excuse that I was mute, and they were not equipped to cope with a mute. It was my parent's first great shame. On the very day that I Guardian Angels, when my mother drug me from the building by my upper arm while I fought against her, I saw the Beast. He was right behind a tree, watching me with his head down and his teeth bared.

I tried to get my mother's attention, but she hissed, "Stop it, stop. Don't you dare embarrass me anymore."

I think she always hated me from that moment on.

No one ever saw the Beast except for me. My parents opted to homeschool me instead of placing me into public kindergarten. They tried to calm me down before putting me back in the world. The isolation seemed to help for a while. I was able to retreat back into myself. Our farm was out in the open - on a field, our closest neighbor was ten miles away. Until I went to Guardian Angels, I thought that my family and I were the only people who existed, and those who went to our church were able to live only then and there on Sunday mornings. While I was being kept at home, everyone else out in the world died and their bodies decomposed before I could see them. We were alone again. I spent my time doodling in a notebook, trying to create an image of that creature - of the monster which plagued me. Haunted me. Yet every time I tried, his figure dissipated from my mind.

My body began to adjust to the bathwater. I allowed my arms to float to the surface, I stared at the straight razor that I stole from my father's bathroom sink. It rested on the rim of the tub.

When I was ten, a Jane Doe was found by my father's friend in a shallow pond a little outside his farm, hovering face-down on the water. Her body was bloated, and decomposition had already taken hold. She was blonde like me, and she had been murdered by her boyfriend. He was a meth cook who lived with her out in the woods. They were both high when he killed her. He had stabbed her in the throat and pushed her through the window of their trailer. It wasn't until he had sobered up that he'd realized what he'd done and took her body to dump in the pond.

My tiny town doesn't have a proper prison, so he was taken to the next largest city. For months, no one talked about anything else. The man's name was Randall Hayman, and he said that the girl was called Estelle Wallace. It was not until the police tried to contact the Wallace family that they realized she did not exist.

Estelle Wallace was a wealthy European widow who had immigrated to Florida in the '60s. While the 'Blonde in the Pond', as people called her, was being murdered, Estelle Wallace was sipping a Mai Tai with other wealthy European widows. Randall Hayman was sentenced to twenty years in prison for the death of the Blonde in the Pond. They pressed him to reveal her true identity. It did not take long for everyone to realize that, to him, she was Estelle Wallace.

People plastered her picture everywhere. Some of the women around town called her their 'sister' and swore they would find out who she was. They felt that it was their sacred duty, but nothing ever came of it. Every town they had been able to track her to find a different name, a different story, a different crime. The more they discovered, the more uncomfortable everyone grew about discussing her. They said she was fallen, a traveling shadow who left a trail of veiled darkness behind her. The town quietly decided to bury her story with her body and her sisters disowned her. She was one of the 'bad women', one of those who had it coming. And thus, the good women had to let her go, lest they be tainted by her tortured existence. She was abandoned and life went on much as it had before. Randall Hayman is still in prison.

Before Jane Doe was forgotten, they had found a grainy picture of her in Hayman's wallet. Her hair was braided back, and she was lying on a bed, resting against a bundle of pillows. She was in the middle of painting her nails blood red when the picture was taken. She had looked up and smiled into the eye of the camera. She had bangs, not cut to the right side like mine, but sliced directly across her forehead. Her hair was frizzy. She was around 140 pounds and they speculated that she was aged between twenty-five and thirty years old. She wore too much eyeliner and pink lipstick. Her face was caked over heavily with foundation. I had always wondered what she would have looked like without makeup. She was wearing a dolman knit sweater made of rayon and worn, pale jeans. Her feet were crossed.

One day at school, instead of creating my dream mansion out of pieces of magazines, I cut her picture out of a newspaper and laminated it. I started carrying it around in a tiny felt purse that had once housed a small stuffed puppy who had been discarded to the other side of my room. The Blonde in the Pond was my first friend. But, slowly, I deserted her just as everyone else did. I forgot her ruby nail polish and her frizzy blonde braid. I forgot how she was thrown in a pond to rot after being stabbed by her lover. I kept her picture though, always under my mattress so my parents wouldn't find it.

The only sound in the bathroom was the splashing of the water in the tub as I shifted toward the wadded-up towel, unraveling it. Her glossy, laminated image flopped out and onto the ground. She stared up at me, questioning. I could almost hear her challenging me: 'Why did you leave? Why come back now?'

I lifted the photo toward me, resting it against a dry spot in the tub. She could see the Beast; she knew him. He had killed her as much as Hayman did. Her eyes held that dark secret which neither of us would ever be able to tell. She had tried to make herself disappear, to become a wisp of smoke that the Beast could not see, could not eat or touch. But he could still smell, that was how he was always able to follow her. She kept running and running, thinking she could outrun him so he wouldn't catch up to her. She was foolish to think that; he would have found her no matter what she had done. Or maybe I was wrong and perhaps he did possess her. Perhaps he ate her soul and whoever she had been before.

My hands quivered as I reached for the straight razor.

"Did it hurt?" I whispered to the photo.

I looked away sharply and I realized how stupid the question was.

She kept staring at me. Her cherry nail polish forever wet.

I wished I could tell her how I loved her, but the words were stuck inside my throat. I wished I could apologize for leaving her alone. I wished I could slit Randal Hayman's throat with the straight razor I stole from my father.

Instead, I said, "I started talking because of you. Part of you absorbed into me. You wouldn't let him take my voice forever. Thank you for that."

I wished I knew her name. I would have given anything to know her name. My fingers swiped across the razor. It gleamed and reflected against the bathwater.

I had always loved taking baths. I had always loved swimming in the summertime and visiting the Floridian oceans during family vacations. The water felt as though I had come home after being away for many years. Our ancestors existed only in the water before they decided to venture onto dry land, our original mistake. I closed my eyes and dipped my head back into the boiling liquid of the bath. At that moment, I believed I could recall the watery place I inhabited within my mother's womb. I began in the water. I would end in the water. There must have been something to that. I had always found it strange that scuba diving gear and astronaut suits were so similar. The first time I swam in the sea was on the coast of Key West. I was twelve. I could still recall dunking my head below the ocean's surface and thinking how that moment would be the closest I would ever come to the moon itself. We began as little more than dust from stars and when this world devours itself and bursts into nothing, we will return to that place in the sky. My eyelids fluttered open, suddenly misted over.

I was in elementary school when I saw the Beast again. For the first few months, I had coped fairly well in a private school designed for disabled children. At that time, my parents never believed I would speak. They had called me slow and told people to talk loudly when they tried to communicate with me.

The Beast came to me while I was on the playground. A young boy had kicked my pet rock down a grassy hill and into a pond. I could still recall the way it splashed. My temper erupted and my eyes vibrated. I wanted to bury my fingers in his hair and rip his skull in half. I could remember lunging toward him and knocking him to the ground. I straddled him and beat against his chest. He began to scream. Some teachers came and tore me off, though not before I had broken his nose. While they dragged me away, I looked over my shoulder and saw the Beast.

He was a mammoth in size, covered in thick white and grey fur. Back then, it was slick and neatly kept. His shoulders were hunched and prominent, and his back sloped down to meet a high pelvis, strong and broad; shaped like a grizzly bear's. His legs were thick around the thighs but funneled near the calves. His paws were colossal, they could spread all across the dirt and grass. I saw his ivory claws from a distance, filthy and sharpened to a point. His head was finely angled, similar to that of a timber wolf, and proportioned to fit his massive body. And his eyes, God help me, were the exact blue as mine.

The moment I saw him, I became quiet and still as though he had cast a spell on me and sent me into slumber. I did not understand how he was devouring me from the inside out. I was too young and confused. Time passed, and as I grew, so did my temper. The Beast's attacks became more frequent. Everything made me furious. Everything was an unforgivable offense. The way someone wore their hair, the tone of their voice, how their jacket fell against their shoulders; it was all too overwhelming. I did not even try to suppress the contempt that I felt. I started talking, and when I entered middle school, I became a vicious bird of prey. Instead of trying to quell the fury that constantly crazed me, I gave myself over to it. I had become his partner. The only time that I was free of his possession was when I danced. In the studio, all that rage died away and I was peaceful. I was gentle. I did not speak much, but I was tender to whom I did. High school came, and I began to realize what had happened to me. A person cannot truly understand that a demon lives within them until the devil has all but slaughtered them completely — pecked away at them from the inside out. There wasn't anyone in my school who was not afraid of me. I was the subject of every college essay — the story of how they overcame me. I served out my punishment by bathing in black loneliness. It felt like being in an underwater cave, floating naked in isolation to protect everyone else.

I threw myself into dance and did what I could to hold out hope that my body would somehow become unbroken. Instead of allowing myself to give in to the Beast's wrath, completely and opening lashing out, I allowed it to fester inside of me. I even left Jane Doe, my one true companion, the only person who could possibly understand what was happening to me. The fury within me felt like a fire, burning and scalding my insides constantly. It throbbed. Every moment was agony. I ached to take a knife and plunge it into a stranger's neckline, to feel some sense of relief. Yet, in my efforts to try and suppress the Beast, I only made him grow. And he grew angrier. I gave him a place to nest inside of my ribs. My lungs became crushed as his girth pressed against them; I could not breathe. His weight was what destroyed my body. He took away my ballet. He knew that was my one defense against him.

I jammed my eyes shut again and pressed my feet against the wall of the tub. My toes splayed out. My feet were so repulsive. The bunions and calluses persisted with a vengeance, and my feet were forever misshapen. The bones themselves were twisted. It was the Beast. He had ruined me for the rest of my days. There would never be a moment when there was not some form of pain, there would never be a moment that there was not a fight to the death against him. I had tried existing without my weapon, without ballet, but it had become unbearable. I looked back up to the window. He had come closer. I brought the razor to my flesh.

"Oh, God, God, oh God," I breathed through gritted teeth.

My heart slammed like a hammer into my temples. I twisted my head and grunted softly. I slid the razor down my left wrist and then my right. Pain sliced into me, and red gushed out and into the clear water. My river of crimson diluted the transparent liquid in the bath.

"Fuck, oh, my God," I whimpered.

"You'll pass out soon, from blood loss. Try not to freak out, you don't want to ruin your last few moments when it won't do any good."

I saw Jane Doe perched on the edge of the bath. Her hair was twisted back in a rope braid, and she brushed ruby polish across her nails. She stared at me and instantly I calmed.

"Okay."

She smiled at me, still painting one nail over and over. "You have the prettiest hair. I always wanted my hair to be that shade of blonde. No matter how I tried to grow it out it never went past my armpits. Lucky." She had a raspy, husky voice.

Blood continued to spill out as I pressed the back of my head against the bathtub wall. "I hate it, it's so heavy. When I danced it took forever to put it up in a bun. When I did it always felt like a growth."

She cocked one eyebrow. "Shit. Why didn't you cut it?"

I stared at her too-light pink lipstick and heavy eyeliner. "I don't know."

I wanted to touch her, but I was afraid that if I did she would vanish like a cloud of fog.

She breathed in and out and asked me gently, "What is it you're doing here, sweetheart? You think you're some kind of rebel?"

"You're one to talk."

She laughed. "You're letting him win, you're giving in."

I could feel the life as it drained away from my body. It slipped from me as masses of blood oozed out. "I'm winning the war. He never thought I'd really do it."

"It's not like you haven't tried before."

"This time it'll work." My eyes watered and my lips quivered as I smiled. "I'll be free."

She stopped painting her nails for a moment.

"Poor little thing," she whispered.

I breathed through my nose. "Don't pity me, please. You and I are the same. Aren't we?"

She ticked her head to the side slightly. "You're too young to be like me. You don't understand death."

My wrists began to throb mercilessly. "God."

"Just relax. You're close now."

A violent pounding slammed against the window. The Beast hurled himself against the glass. He howled. He screamed and clawed.

"See? You see? He knows I beat him," I said as darkness began to tunnel my vision.

Jane Doe did not even look up at the window. "Or maybe he's celebrating."

"I'm so tired."

The banging continued. I sat in a pool of blood.

Jane Doe reached down. Her fingertips almost touched the water. "Don't be such a stranger, sweetheart."

The violent drumming reached a fervor, and I felt my eyelids flutter closed. I was so tired. I tried to shut myself away from the sound. I tried to let go.

"Break it! Now! Break it down!" A scream from outside the door.

I heard a crackling snap, like wood being smashed and shattered. A waft of cold air flowed up to me. It washed over the surface of the bath and my face. The pounding ceased.

"Oh, Jesus. Oh, my God," my sister's frantic voice cried.

My head flopped over in her direction. My lips were unable to form coherent words.

"Get a robe. Get a robe! Call 911," Maggie shouted.

My eyes pried themselves open, and the blurry image of my father came into view. I saw his grey hair flip as his head turned toward the door. He seized my white bathrobe from its hook. I heard myself moan.

"I know, baby. I know. I know. It'll be okay," Maggie said.

He fumbled towards her and threw the robe down to the ground. "Calm down, you're not helping anyone by panicking."

I felt her cold fingers as they reached around my submerged torso. I was pulled from the warmth and safety of my bath. The warm water cascaded away from my flesh as I broke the surface tension. I curled my legs up. My head fell back from the weight of my hair.

"Hello? Hi, this is Kurt, out on Marion road. I'm afraid my daughter's done it again. There's blood everywhere. No, she's still breathing. She seems confused. Yes, she's awake."

My limbs tumbled over the wall of the tub and my sister dropped me onto the icy tile. My thighs and pelvis squeaked as I hit the ground.

"Stop the bleeding, got to stop the bleeding," my sister muttered.

"They're sending an ambulance," my father said.

"Got to stop the bleeding."

"Tom Kentworth was the one who'll come. You remember Tom? He was at the MaClaine's Thanksgiving party. They'll be here in five minutes. They told me to keep her awake."

"Why are you always so fucking melodramatic?" she sobbed.

"There's no need for cursing, Margaret," my father said.

"Oh, my God, oh, my God."

"The Lord won't listen if you disrespect him," he said.

The soft fabric of the robe wrapped over my body. It stuck to the slick wetness of my skin.

"No," I managed. "No, no, no."

Maggie sniffled as she tightened the robe around me. "Shut up, you brat. Christ, you're unbelievable."

"Margaret. I absolutely won't allow that kind of language in my house."

"Get bandages, dad."

"I don't know where the bandages are."

"Go outside and get mom, she'll know where the first aid is."

"The ambulance will be here soon."

"Dad."

"You're not doing anyone any good by panicking. She'll be fine. She's done this before, and she was fine then, too. Don't you remember the thing with the pills?"

"This is different. Go find mom."

"She'll hear the sirens and come inside."

"God, dad," she wailed. "Oh, my God."

"Margaret. For the last time, don't say His name in vain."

Darkness encased me. It shrouded me in a veil as my entire being went limp, and I slept.

The next time I felt myself breathing, it smelled like antiseptic and warm blankets. There was a prickling weight against the inside of my elbow. My chest and torso were covered in a scratchy fabric. My arms were at my sides. My head was propped up, my feet were bare. My eyelids were crusted over, but they pried apart as a dim light hit them. I craned my neck down and saw that my wrists were covered in white gauze. My chest tightened. I sat up, and I felt that my hair had been braided and pushed to the side. I began to breathe heavily as I realized where I was.

I was alive. I was at the hospital. I was in a bed and I was alive. There was an IV strapped to my arm and my wrists were bandaged and I was alive.

"Hello?" I shouted shakily.

I heard the clicking of heels. A nurse rounded the corner and leaned her head into my room. She smiled when she saw me.

"Hello, honey. We didn't expect you to be awake so soon. Your mother and sister are in the cafe. Your father was here, but he had to go back home to feed your chickens. I'll be back in just a moment."

Her heels clicked back outside and I heard her walking back down the hall. I did not move as I waited for her to return. I wanted to collapse back onto the bed, but I would not let myself. It did not take long for the clicking to multiply and echo through the halls.

My mother's form appeared in the doorway. Her brown hair was bundled up into a knot at the back of her head. She wore slacks and a jacket with floral embroidery. Her hands were laced at the bottom of her torso. Her jaw was pushed to the side. Her blue eyes were icy and chilled as she stared down at me. At that moment, I realized that I had gone too far. She could chalk up the pills to a psychological break. It could be hidden from the rest of the county. 'Dancer's drama,' is what she told everyone. It was almost romantic, à la Natalie Portman in *Black Swan*. But this was messy. I had ruined the white microfiber robe she had purchased for me last Christmas. Unforgivable. Ever since I was banished from Guardian Angels, my hands had been against her shoulder blades and I had been pushing her, slowly, from the edge of a great cliff that dropped into a frigid ocean. This had been the final shove. She was already floating in the water, dead from hypothermia.

"Really, what *were* you thinking?" she asked me, not stepping any closer to my bed.

Maggie suddenly pushed past her and rushed into the room. Her hair was down to her shoulders - not tied up in its usual ponytail. She looked so much older than when I last saw her. There was a spot of dried, crusted blood on her tennis shoes. She breathed out and pressed a hand against her chest.

"Thank the Lord," she said.

She made the sign of the cross with her middle and index finger. My mother did the same. I did not know what to say. I wanted to leap across the bed and peel every inch of Maggie's skin and flesh away until there was nothing left but bone, yet I also had to stop myself from rolling onto the floor and crawling toward her to press my lips against her bloody tennis shoes. A bubbling rose in my chest which transformed into spasms that took control of me. Water gushed down my cheeks as ugly sobs contorted my face. Maggie's expression melted into an affectionate gaze. She wrapped herself around my body. Her shoulder pressed against my throat. I realized then that she was the one who had braided my hair. I placed my hands against her back. My fingertips pushed against her spine.

"You're alright now, baby. You're safe, you're safe. I forgive you."

I began to dig my nails deeper into her as my teeth clenched. "Why didn't you let me go?"

I felt her stiffen beneath my grip. "What?"

Fury overtook me. I wanted to destroy her. "I was almost free. I almost got away."

She moved to wriggle away from me, but my grip kept her locked down.

"Stop. What are you doing? Stop it," she gasped.

My hands traveled up her shoulders and closer toward her neck. "I wasn't going to hurt anyone anymore."

"Stop it," she commanded.

"He wasn't going to hurt me anymore."

"Lily, stop it!"

"I was getting away," I screamed. I scrambled to wrap my fingers around her throat.

Two sets of hands grabbed me and pushed me down onto my bed. My mother and the nurse. I flailed against them. I thrashed and flung myself away from their grip. I saw my sister's face contort into a mask of terror. She kept her hands at her side and backed away slowly.

I heard her whisper my name.

"I was almost free." I sobbed, slamming my head against the back wall while trying to relieve myself from my mother and the nurse.

I was dead, yet I was alive. I wanted to rip my flesh off and allow my skeleton to burst into the fluorescent lighting. But I was locked in a cage whose key was swallowed by the Beast.

I was nothing.

I was caged.

A pain penetrated my inner elbow. I twisted my head and saw the silver end of a needle pushing into my skin. It did not take long for my head to start swimming. My body began to relax as I was submerged back into the bath. I felt every breath as it entered and left my chest. I slumped against the pillow. My braid pressed against the back of my head as my eyelids fluttered closed.

Chapter 6
The Present, Lorelai

Lily's eyes focused on her sneakers. She knew The Doctor's eyes were on her, but she refused to meet his gaze. Shame barred her from doing so.

"Well, dear," he said. "How do you feel after your second session of hypnotherapy?"

Her back ached. "I'm tired. But I'm always tired."

"Yes. It's a process. But you are doing so well, just fantastic. I'm very proud of you."

She almost laughed.

There was a swift rapping on the door. She snapped her head toward the sound.

The Doctor's shoulders clenched up. "Sorry, dear. Just a moment."

He rose from his chair and unlatched the door. Nurse Kathy stood in the frame of the entrance. Her hands were laced in front of her. "So sorry, Doctor, but it's 2:00. Seraphina is here to take Lily for her ride. Should I tell her to come back later?"

A flower bloomed within Lily's stomach, sprouting up to tickle the inside of her throat. She sat up straight in her chair. "No, I want to go."

The Doctor spun around. "I'm not sure that's a good idea. I hate to interrupt our time together, especially since I feel we've only just begun to make progress. But I suppose our session has gone on longer than expected.

Still, I feel uncomfortable allowing you to leave at this moment. I believe we had just reached a crucial point in your treatment."

"But I —"

"Doctor," Nurse Kathy said. "Don't you think the session could continue afterward? Perhaps a little break would do her some good."

The Doctor hummed under his breath. "Well, I suppose that might be true. Alright, Lily, go on. I'll check in after you're done with the ride."

She bolted up so quickly that her back cramped from the movement. She rushed toward the door and out into the hallway without looking back at The Doctor. Little sparks flared up under her skin and made sweat break out on her palms and under her armpits.

"Wait, you need to put on a scarf. Or at least some gloves." Nurse Cathy called out as she flew toward the doorway.

Lily did not respond.

The cold rushed across her skin as she left the building. It cooled her flushed body and washed over her in a wave. Seraphina was leaning up against a tree, her arms intertwined and wrapped around her stomach. The wind blew her ringlet curls back behind her. She offered Lily a small smile.

"Still aren't cold?"

Lily shook her head. "No, no. I'm fine."

"You're strong," Seraphina said.

Lily gestured toward her. "You're not wearing much again, either."

"Living on top of a mountain will kill you if you can't get used to this kind of weather."

Lily laughed, too loudly. "No doubt."

Seraphina flipped her gaze toward the two horses tied up behind them. "Pixie has been missing you."

Lily's eyes remained fixed on her as she boarded Pharaoh. She accomplished the action in one swift movement, barely restrained by the cold or by gravity. Her olive skin and honey brown eyes caught the wispy light and contrasted against the white snow. Lily was sure there had never been anything more beautiful; the oceans, the mountains, the stars, they all paled in comparison to her. She wondered what Seraphina's full lips must have tasted like.

"How are you today?" Lily asked.

"Not bad. You?"

"I'm good. It's good to see you again."

"It's good to see you too, faerie."

Lily melted, her body began to tingle. "Where are we going?"

"I thought we'd go up to Lorelai Mountain. That's where I live. There's a really pretty overlook I think you'd like."

Lily's stomach sank. "Lorelai?"

Seraphina grasped Pharaoh's reins tighter. "Yeah. Why?"

"No reason."

Seraphina made a clicking noise with her tongue and teeth that signaled for Pharaoh to move forward. Lily followed suit with Pixie.

"What's wrong? You seem nervous."

Lily tried to keep her voice from trembling. "I grew up a little way from here. People always used to say that Lorelai Mountain was haunted."

Seraphina stared at her for a moment before smiling slightly.

"I should have guessed. God, that's funny."

"I'm sorry if I said anything -"

"No! No, of course not. Tell me what they say. I'd like to know."

Lily adjusted in her saddle. "They say that people disappear there, all the time. Don't you remember the story of that kid? The one who was dumped and froze to death? No one knew who he was or where he came from."

"Yeah, Sebastian."

"What?"

62

"I don't know much about him either," she continued. "Sometimes I see him though, in dreams or when it's late at night. A few years ago, he told me his name. I think he gets lonely sometimes. And I think he's scared of being forgotten."

"Did he...did he tell you what happened to him?"

Seraphina's eyes fell downward. "No. I just feel his pain. It's the pain of a child who can't find his parents."

"You aren't scared of him?"

"Oh no, of course not. But I guess I can understand why most people are. The Mountain is unforgiving."

Lily watched her. "There's nothing about this place that frightens you?"

She glanced back over to Lily. "I don't know. I was born on Lorelai. My mother raised me on it. Maybe that's why. But it is true, people disappear on the Mountain all the time. I've never been quite sure what it is. Maybe it's the wolves or the bears, but I doubt that. More than anything else, I'd imagine it's the cold, hunger, just exposure. Lorelai is pretty fucking brutal if you aren't prepared for it. There are hardly any pathways, it's so easy to get lost. Some nights, if you can't find shelter by the time the sun goes down, you're on borrowed time. I've almost frozen to death myself once or twice."

"Why do you stay there?" Lily said.

"It's my home. I'm one of the very lucky few who know exactly where they belong. I have my horses, my dogs, my cats. My dream is to start a sanctuary on Lorelai, maybe one for bears; my family owns a big plot of land a little farther down the Mountain. It'd be the perfect spot."

Lily flickered her eyes between Seraphina the snowy landscape before them. "You don't get lonely?"

"Until two years ago, my mother lived with me. I wasn't lonely then, sometimes it even felt cramped."

"What happened to her? Did she leave?"

She nudged Pharaoh's side gently, and the horse sped up. Lily did the same.

"She got restless, tired of being in the same place. She was going crazy, she had to leave. She offered to take me with her, but it was time for us to let go of each other."

"Do you know where she went?"

Seraphina clicked her tongue again. "I know she was heading towards Tibet. I got a postcard from Lhasa a little while ago, she'd always wanted to hike through the Himalayas. If I had to take a guess, I'd imagine that's where she is. Sometimes I miss her, sometimes I miss her so badly I think I'll go crazy. But I go into town to get supplies and talk to the people there when I can, it helps me get out of my head. Mostly the animals keep me sane, especially the horses."

Lily wanted so desperately to tell Seraphina how beautiful she looked as the snow fell into her hair. She tightened her fingers around Pharaoh's mane. Her chest began to ache. Her mouth felt swollen. Lily tried to swallow. Her tongue burned with the desire to confess.

Lily examined her. She could feel the heat radiating off of her skin and eyes and fingertips. Seraphina's flames were not blistering within her, they did not sear the flesh from her bones as Lily's did. Her fire was a smooth light that kept her from freezing to death in the harsh mountain winter. She could ignite or extinguish it whenever it suited her. She understood it, and it understood her. They moved together in perfect unison. Nothing was burned. Lily wanted to feel that warmth.

"Any reason you're staring at me?" Seraphina suddenly asked, smiling to expose her gums.

"What?" Lily gasped stupidly. "Sorry. God, Sorry."

Seraphina grinned again with her lips pressed together tightly, the left corner of her mouth raised higher than the right. "Don't be sorry."

Lily's face became dewey with sweat.

Seraphina sighed then. "God, you're pretty."

A wave of ecstasy made Lily's skin tingle. "No."

"I think you are."

"I danced as the Firebird once, by Stravinsky. I had so much makeup on, I think I might have been pretty then. Just that one time." Lily tried to laugh.

"I wish I could have seen you dance. Were you ever in *Swan Lake*?"

Lily nodded.

Seraphina faced back toward the snowy landscape. "It's cliché, but that's always been my favorite. I love the music, especially when Odette dies. That's a little morbid, isn't it?"

Lily's heart plummeted. "I wasn't the lead. I danced the Four Little Swans, that's really the only thing I did. And I tore my Achilles so bad it never recovered."

"I'm sorry. No way in hell could I have been a ballerina." Seraphina drew in a slow breath, allowing it to drip out of her mouth. "Isn't it lovely out here? I still love the snow."

Lily's eyes swept over the terrain. She had not realized how deeply they had gone into the woods. The sky had morphed into a darker shade of silver, and it became increasingly difficult to distinguish the snow on the ground from the clouds.

"Yeah, it's nice."

Seraphina cleared her throat.

Out of the corner of Lily's eye, she saw her fidgeting on Pharaoh.

"Can I ask you something?" Seraphina said.

Lily looked back to her fully, all at once flooded with apprehension. "Sure, okay."

Seraphina's fingers ticked around Pharaoh's neck as she petted her.

"I haven't been able to stop thinking about you since we met. I don't know what's wrong with me, maybe I'm just being weird. And I don't even know if you're into girls, but…I don't know. I'm not any good at this."

Lily almost melted into her saddle. "Are you serious?"

"Sorry. Forget I said anything."

Lily's breathing staggered in her chest. She pulled on Pixie's reins, stopped both herself and the horse in their tracks. "No, no. I think you're wonderful. I've just been so terrified of you. I feel like I haven't been able to breathe since I last saw you."

Seraphina's eyes fixed on her as Pharaoh's hooves came to a stop.

The gravity of what she said sunk into Lily's flesh and brain, her cheeks and eyes grew hot.

Seraphina's gaze softened. "Let's tie up the horses here. We're close to what I wanted to show you."

Lily swallowed a wad of saliva. It clawed its way down her throat like sandpaper. She nibbled on her bottom lip as it quivered, shakily lowering herself down and onto the snowy ground. She blinked away water while fasting Pixie's reins to a tree branch. She felt a warm palm rest on her shoulder. She shuddered, a burst of light beamed through her veins.

Lily spun around, trying to block her red eyes from Seraphina's gaze. "Did I do it right?"

Seraphina glanced over her shoulder. "Perfect. You're perfect. Come on, walk with me."

Lily obeyed and moved quietly behind Seraphina. She crossed her arms over her chest, rubbing her limbs up and down.

"I'm cold," Lily said, almost in a whisper.

Seraphina turned around. "You should've worn a coat after all."

"You still aren't? Cold, I mean?"

Seraphina shook her head. "How many times do I have to tell you, faerie? I don't get cold anymore. Chilled, maybe, but not cold."

They traveled in silence together, their shoulders almost touching, but not quite.

Lily clenched her teeth, desperate for something to say. "Ever seen *The Deer Hunter?*"

"The one with Christopher Walken? And Robert De Niro?"

Lily nodded. "Yeah."

"I don't know. I think maybe I did, a long time ago."

"I think about the scene when Michael shoots the buck all the time. It was always my dad's favorite movie. I used to hate it. I still have nightmares about that deer's face when it panics, when it realizes that it's about to die. Its mouth fell open, its eyes darted around. I remember seeing it for the first time when I was thirteen." Lily swiped her tongue across her dry lips. "They didn't shoot it in real life, they used a tranquilizer."

The hush resumed as they continued through the snow. They moved toward an edge of the mountain; a cliff overlooking the end of their world. Lily's jaw flung open as they made their way to see over its side.

"Oh, my God," she breathed.

Misty clouds hung low over the jagged tops of mountains below them. Snow blanketed the pine trees, sparkling in the dim, soft light. Wind rushed gently down the low slopes, singing in a quiet hum. Lily closed her eyes and allowed the cold to nip and bite at her chilled flesh. She put her palms up as the wind brushed up behind her.

"I wish you could see this during the summer when the snow melts," Seraphina said.

Lily opened her eyes again. "I think it's beautiful the way it is now."

She heard Seraphina shuffle, inching closer to her. "Can I touch you? Can I hold your hand?"

Lily blinked rapidly, a shiver passing through her spine. "Yes."

Seraphina's fingertips moved over Lily's knuckles, then slid underneath her palm.

"Can I kiss you?"

Lily almost whimpered. Her fingers and toes numbed.

"I've never kissed anyone before."

"Could I be your first, then? I mean, we don't have to do anything you don't want to do."

Lily turned to look at her fully. "I won't be good at it."

Seraphina reached up to press her palm against Lily's cheek. "You're so beautiful."

Lily trembled, stepping closer to her. She swallowed loudly, running her quivering fingers through Seraphina's spiral curls without another thought.

"You're beautiful."

Seraphina pushed her forehead forward until their hairlines were pressed together.

"Do you want me to kiss you?" she whispered.

"Yes. Yes," Lily gasped gently.

She felt Seraphina's warm breath hit her mouth in short, warm puffs. Seraphina cupped the back of Lily's head. The air around them stilled, and Lily's heart palpitated as what felt like two pieces of soft velvet pressed against her raw, scabbed lips. She levitated, moaning softly as she wrapped her arms around Seraphina's torso. It was instinctive. She wanted to touch every part of her as her fingers reached under Seraphina's sweater. The other girl's skin was silken and smooth, warm against Lily's hand. Seraphina pressed her pelvis into her's. Passion and light poured into her in a way she'd never before experienced. Just as their lips opened and their tongues began to twist around each other, a violent flash snapped her brain like a whip. Lily gasped as their mouths were still pressed together. Her eyelids burst open. Her soul was ripped from her body, and she drifted away, through the clouds and up into the stratosphere.

Chapter 7
The Future, After

My breathing was shallow, low, and almost silent. I sensed the weight of my arms as they laid crossed over my chest. My body was heavy. I felt my heart pound furiously in my chest.

Seraphina and I used to camp out in this cabin during the summer for a month or two. We would leave the sanctuary in the hands of someone we trusted and disappear into the forest. Seraphina loved the way the trees flowered there, and she loved the silence. There were times when I hated the cabin and there were times that I felt it was my paradise. The air had always been warmer there than in the mountains. Last summer, I had not come with her to the cabin. I had felt smothered and locked in with her. I could not tell if she had felt the same. She and I had been two mice trapped in a cage that was too small for both of us, so we fought and clawed until one of us ate the other. No matter the victor, they ended up scarred, torn, and bloody.

I did not allow my eyes to depart from the stag mounted on the cabin wall. I did not know exactly when she had shot it. It must have been this past summer when she had gone there alone. I pressed my fingers into my arm, digging my nails into my flesh until the skin turned white and red-rimmed. The stag stared back at me. Its marbled eyes were cold and stiff. I could feel the betrayal - the confusion in its stuffed face. Seraphina had promised me that she would quit deer hunting after

I had moved in. She had even stopped eating meat for a while. Yet she had always told me that deer hunting was a natural part of the circle of life, population control. She would take out one of the sick ones, 'for the good of the rest of the herd,' she would always say. She would eat the meat and skin the animal herself, she would use every part of the creature that she could. I had understood, but something in me could never allow it. I could recall the fit I had over her hunting, crying and wailing and screaming at her that it was me she was killing. She had loved me enough to give in to me back then.

I ripped a hole out of the inside of my lip. Blood seeped underneath my tongue. God knew she had done it on purpose. She meant for me to see it. Punishment for leaving her. She would never forgive me for being the one to leave. She would never forget all the deer that escaped her gun because of me. I swallowed a wad of saliva that felt like dust and metal scraping down my throat. I reached up. My fingertips just barely rubbed against the deer's fur.

Then, a short rap suddenly came against the door. I gasped and whipped around.

I placed my fingers on the doorknob, twisting it open. A squeak penetrated the air as the door swung open. A low meow caught my attention. I looked down and saw a small black figure look up at me with bright, yellow eyes that contrasted against the darkness of the forested night. Relief flooded through me as I smiled down at the black cat.

"Ichabod," I whispered, balling my hand into a fist.

I lowered my fist, allowing the cat to sniff my knuckles. I remembered first seeing him three summers ago. He had been younger and smaller then. His eyes used to be brighter. I begged Seraphina to take him home, but she was adamant in her refusal.

"He's wild," I remembered her telling me. "He'd be miserable, locked in the house."

"He'll freeze in the winter," I had told her.

Then she had sighed and put her hand to my face. "He'd rather die than live his life in captivity."

Ichabod purred and pressed his head into my fist.

"I never imagined you'd make it this long."

We used to store dry cat food in a cupboard. I left the door open and stepped forward into the kitchen. I swung open the cabinet above the sink. A bag of cat food pellets sat waiting, covered in a thin layer of dust. I plucked a small bowl away from the clean dishes and scooped out a bundle of kibble with my hand. I dumped it in the dish with a clatter. I moved through the cold, wooden floor in my bare feet. My legs were so iced over that I could hardly feel my gray sweatpants as they rubbed against my thighs and calves. I placed the bowl of food out on the front stoop. Ichabod had already wandered off. I knew he would be back. I doubt I would see him, but the dish would be empty by morning.

I shut the door and allowed my gaze to flit about the house; at the furnishings which remained exactly as they were for decades. I gazed at the ancient couch covered in floral fabric, then at the stained carpet which may have been white many years ago. I stared at the wicker chairs and flattened cushions that rested in their seats. I stared at the photos fixed to the wall of Ramsey family members I would never know. Seraphina inherited the cabin from her mother, and it had endured just as her mother had left it to endure. I wondered if Seraphina would ever alter it. She had always said she wanted to. I took a deep breath inward and flipped my head to the right. I caught an image of myself in a musty mirror, caked over on the edges with grime.

I was growing old.

I moved closer to the mirror and pressed my fingertips into my jawline. Thirty-seven years old. I had been twenty-one a year ago. The first era of my life had passed. I wondered if my parents ever wondered where I had gone, why I had never come home after they took me to Meadowlark. The only news I ever had of my family was a Christmas card from Maggie where my sister posed with her five children. Her latest baby was less than a year at the time. I knew exactly where my parents still were, on the chicken farm at the foot of the mountains. Perhaps I could never forgive them. Perhaps they could never forgive me. My mother had always seemed so stagnant at thirty-seven, but it was a tranquil stagnation. She had lived a respectable life, carved into her flesh and brain by her mother and their mothers before them. The only thing which was impure in her life had been me, and it had been many years since I plagued her.

I suppose I always thought I would end up like my mother. But I had never been my mother. But I had never borne any resemblance to my mother save for the way we both aged. I rubbed a hand over my braid. It traced down my spine in a rope, reaching down past my breasts. I pursed my lips, twisting my body to the side. I moved to smooth my palm over my belly. It no longer had the swift flatness that it once did. I breathed in sharply. I ate all the time, and I enjoyed food. It felt good to enjoy food. I wondered what that meant. I jolted violently in shock as the telephone rang. I quickly plucked the phone from the receiver and pressed it onto my ear.

"Yes?" I answered.

The line was silent, save for gentle static.

"I'm sorry, I can't hear you. I have terrible service out here."

Pieces of a voice splintered through the phone.

"I'm sorry, again, but I think I'm going to have to hang up now," I said loudly.

"Lily?" the voice finally asked, the sound all at once crystalline and sharp.

"Yes?" I said quietly in reply.

"Lily. It's good to hear from you. So good."

"I'm sorry, who is this?"

"It's so good to hear you talk. I've always loved the way you speak."

"I'm sorry. I know your voice, but I can't place it."

The voice grew quiet. A light scoff pierced my eardrum. "Ah. Yes. Well, I suppose you think that's good. You've been happy, haven't you?"

My eyes flickered over the strained carpet floor. "Who are you?"

"Can I come over?"

My heart burned in my chest. "The reception is terrible. I don't think we're understanding each other."

"No."

"Who is this?"

"I'm coming over. You don't have to let me in if you don't want to."

"Tell me who you are."

The line emitted a sharp click. My eyelids fluttered and dizziness overtook me as I looked down at the phone. I pushed it back onto the receiver. My hand lingered over the device.

I knew that voice. I had known it all my life. Why could I not remember? I looked out to the window. The midnight darkness was overwhelming. Nothing existed there except for Ichabod and me. It was an entirely separate dimension, split away from the place Seraphina and I used to inhabit; Ichabod and I were the only ones who knew. The difference between the black cat and myself is that he knew how to travel in shadows, he knew how to see in the night. I looked down at the couch where my plush white swan sat perched on one of the cushions. It was one of the few things I had taken from the house when I left. Its feathered fur had become slightly yellowed, the twinkling plastic eyes had dulled. I stepped forward, coiling my fingers around the swan's neck. As I bent down, I pressed my lips right next to where its ear would be.

"Are you going to kill me?" I asked in a whisper.

The soft pounding of a fist merged gently with the outside of the door. I moved my hand away from the swan, grasping the end of my braid.

"Yes? Who is it?"

The voice from the telephone radiated from the other side of the door, "I said I was coming. I won't stay long. I just want to say 'hello.'"

"I told you on the phone, I don't know who you are. I'm sorry, but I just, I don't remember."

The voice was silent for a moment. "I see."

An ill-feeling rose in my stomach, and I found myself right at the edge of the door. "Just tell me your name. How do you know me? How did you find me?"

I could very nearly feel the voice's breath from outside. "Perhaps I should just go."

My heart lurched as adrenaline coursed through me. "No, wait."

I flung open the door just as the figure turned his back to me, readying to walk away.

The night wind made my arms rough with risen gooseflesh. I crossed my arms over my shirt. "It's chilly out here. Aren't you cold?"

The figure turned around on his heels, he grinned at me as the wind swirled his hair. "Look at you. It's been such a long time, hasn't it?"

My body flooded with a wave of memory that refused to reach my brain. "Yes. I suppose so. Aren't you cold?"

He tilted his head to the side, his hands stuffed lightly into his pockets. "I'm used to the way the night feels. I have such a hard time with sunshine, remember? My skin is so sensitive."

"Do you want to come in? I can make us a pot of tea."

He scanned me. His eyes brimmed over with affection. He seemed so genuine, so gentle and soothing. Yet, there was something burning and penetrating in his gaze; like a hawk readying itself to swoop down on its prey.

"That would be lovely. It's been so long since anyone invited me in."

I swallowed. The gulping sound was too loud. "Sure, yeah."

He passed me and glided smoothly into the cabin. He smelt achingly fresh, bright, like falling snow on iced-over winter mornings. He wore all black. His hair was colored a gentle chestnut brown. His skin was too pale, as though he truly was allergic to daylight. Yet, when I looked at him, I did not see anything. His face was fully nondescript, lacking any significant features that would exist in a normal human face. It did not feel right to have my eyes fall over him, even for a moment.

"Do you have any Jasmine tea?"

"I only have lotus tea, lotus blossom green tea, I think it's called."

He hummed quietly. "Lovely, that sounds lovely. The lotus is such a beautiful flower."

"How did you get here? How did you find me, all the way out here?"

He slipped off his coat. "I'll always find you. You never asked questions like that before."

I felt him slither through my veins, slowly inflecting me. I knew him, I had forgotten him.

"Sit down," I said.

He remained standing for a moment before finally lowering himself onto one of the chairs, right beside my swan. He gestured to the plush creature. "Who's this?"

My eyes flashed between the man and the swan. "My friend."

"You have a friend? Introduce me, please? What's its name?"

I moved to sit in the loveseat parallel to his. "I don't know. I don't think I ever gave her a name. It was a gift from my sister, a Christmas present."

He smiled at me. "That's hardly acceptable. Any friend of yours is too special to go without a name."

I tried to resist the small grin as it lurched up onto my lips. "Oh? What would you suggest?"

"You could go with Odette, or Odile if you're feeling clever."

I looked into the swan's sparking, beaded eyes. "I never danced the lead in *Swan Lake*. You know that."

"I know."

I looked down at my nails. "I'm not a swan."

"No?"

"No."

"Why say that?"

I chuckled and glanced back up at him. "Because it's true."

"I don't know that that's the case."

"Swans are too pretty."

His eyes fell just beyond my shoulder. "Swans are vicious. Swans have tempers, swans bite. They hiss the way snakes hiss. They're snakes with wings. Haven't you ever seen *The Threatened Swan* by Jan Asselijn?"

I laughed. The vibrating sound ripped from my chest. "So, you're calling me a snake?"

"With wings.".

I laughed again, louder, and with an echo. "Fuck you."

I remembered now the way his presence always made a burst of warmth flower in my stomach, the way a body suddenly warms right before it freezes to death.

"Perhaps you ought to stick with the flower theme. You're Lily, the swan can be Rose, something like that?"

I leaned back in my chair. "I've never liked roses. They smell too sweet. The scent reminds me of a rotting animal melting on asphalt."

He pressed his right index and middle fingers to his lips. "Roses remind you of roadkill?"

"I've never liked roses."

He laced his fingers together. "Fine. What's your favorite flower then? I know you like flowers."

"Yes. I do."

"But you don't like roses."

"I've never cared for flowers," he said. "They make my throat itch and my nose run. And so many of them are too delicate, a snowstorm destroys them. But what's your favorite flower if not the rose?"

I paused for a moment. "You don't remember? I thought you'd remember that."

"No. What's your favorite flower?"

Suddenly, I felt a sense of power over him. "Dandelions. I love dandelions."

"When they're yellow or once they've turned into those white, fully puffs?"

"Both. I don't think there's a more stunning color than yellow dandelions when they flower. And I've never seen anything more freeing than those white seeds when they float away in the wind."

"Dandelions are weeds."

I felt a gentle fire licking at the inside of my stomach. I swallowed it, pouring water on it until it suffocated.

"They're only weeds because people can't control them."

"And because they're common. They're ugly."

"They're common because they've learned how to survive in the wild. Everyone tries to destroy them, but nobody can."

"Do I sense a forced metaphor?"

I coiled my braid around my open palm. "I'll name the swan Dandelion, then."

"Good choice."

"Dandelion."

The voice was suddenly quiet. He grew stock still as he assessed her. "Do you miss dancing? Do you miss being Dandelion for the audience?"

I let the back of my head fall against the loveseat cushion. "It was never just about the audience."

"Still," he replied. "Do you miss it?"

I met his gaze. "In certain ways. I miss the way it felt when I was on pointe. I miss what I could do in those shoes. I miss the resentful, earnest little family I'd make with the other dancers. I don't miss the pain, or how my feet bled. I don't miss the competition. I don't miss how skinny I had to be. I don't miss starving myself. I don't miss the way my back cramped after rehearsal. I miss being a ballerina, I don't miss what it took to get there. I miss the Firebird, the way she felt within me,"

"That's not really an answer."

"Do you still want tea? I think I do."

"That would be wonderful, thank you."

In the kitchen, relief cooled me. I was calm. The farther away I was from him, the more awake I became. I saw him rise out of the corner of my eye, walking over to my music selection.

"Who's your favorite singer?" he called.

"Freddie Mercury."

"What?" he said, clearly surprised.

I filled the electric kettle with water. "Who were you expecting?"

"David Bowie, of course," he said. "Bowie was always your favorite when you were young."

"He never was, not really."

"When did that happen? I never thought… was it because of *Under Pressure*? Is that when you switched? Is that why?"

I betrayed him.

I placed the tea bags into the cups. "I liked the idea of David Bowie, but Freddie was special."

The water bubbled from inside of the kettle. I heard him rustling in the other room. "Could I play *Space Oddity*? For old time's sake?"

I poured scalding hot water into the cups. "Play *Life on Mars?*, it's a better song."

"Fine. Alright."

The introduction to the music began as I carried the mugs by their handles. "Freddie Mercury and the rest of Queen were an immaculate combination. Some of their songs are almost perfect."

"Bowie was an icon, a legend."

"So was Freddie. He had a stronger voice, more stage presence."

"They're two different people. Totally different. They're not comparable, it's stupid to even try."

I sat the cups down on our opposing end-tables. "His voice could be raw, or it could be breathy and kind of ethereal. He was otherworldly, he was unique. There'll never be anybody else like him, not even David Bowie."

"Can we change the subject?"

"Why is this making you so upset?"

His vague eyes found their way back to mine. "Why are you so different now?"

"What?"

"You've changed," he said. "You aren't the way I remember, the way you were before. We got along so well then. I knew everything about you, we had so many things in common. It's hard to talk to you now."

"We remember those times differently."

He stroked his palm over his brown-haired scalp. "You've just forgotten, that's all. When you remember, everything will go back to the way it was."

"What if I can't remember? What if I don't want to?"

He glanced up at the mounted stag head. "Strange custom, keeping a trophy of death. Don't tell me you're the one who shot it. You can't have changed that much."

My heart chilled in my chest. "Seraphina."

"Yes. Of course. How are you doing, by the way? With the separation?"

I crunched down on my lower lip. "I don't know. I'm...numb. I don't think it's quite...I don't know what to do. I don't know how to feel anything."

"You're in shock. Anyone could understand that."

My breathing became staggered. "Your tea is going to get cold."

"How did it end? How did things end between the two of you?"

"Things ended for us a while ago."

"But why leave now?"

"I was suffocating. I needed air, I needed to find a way to breathe again."

"You don't love her anymore?"

"I love her more than anyone in my life. More than anything."

"Then why did you leave? Explain it to me, I don't understand."

"Because I couldn't exist with her anymore," I snapped as I nearly choked on my words.

"What does that mean?"

"I don't know. I just couldn't stand her, and me, I couldn't stand us together."

He began to pace around the room. "And her? How does she feel about you leaving?"

"She hates that I was the one to go instead of her."

He gestured up to the stag head. "Is that why she did this?"

My eyes met with the stag's marbles. "Did what?"

"She knew what this meant, didn't she?"

My breath came out in hot puffs through my nose as my lips parted. "Yes."

"Feisty thing, isn't she?"

"She is, yeah."

"What'll you do?"

"Hum?'

His fingers twitched. "I mean, what do you plan on doing with yourself now? You spent all that time on that fucking mountain with those beasts you 'rescued', what will you do now that you aren't living with those bears and such?"

"I loved those bears."

"Oh, yes?" he questioned sarcastically.

"I grew to love them."

"Yes."

"Maybe I could find work at a different rescue, something like that. I have experience now."

"Would that make you happy?"

"Happiness might be aiming a little high."

"Will it content you, then?"

I crossed my arms over my chest, rubbing them up and down. "Maybe I'll just take a little time. Some time for myself, it's been years since I've been alone. I have some money."

"You miss loneliness?"

"Being alone isn't the same thing as loneliness."

"For you it is."

"It *used* to be."

He scoffed at me. "You just said that you haven't been alone in years, how would you know? This self-awareness you think you possess is a sham. I know you, angel. You may like Freddie Mercury and fucking dandelions, but nothing's changed. You still that same, crazy little girl from the chicken farm."

I had to quell the vibrating anger which threatened to erupt in my chest. "I'm not like when we used to know each other. I'm not how I was. You can't do anything about that. You can't make me the way I was then. Understood? You don't know me anymore."

"I know you."

"You knew me once."

"Then I'll know you again," he said. "You won't just throw me out, not this time."

I stared at him for a moment, forcing my breath to remain steady.

My eyes cut down to his mug, still untouched on the table. "Your tea is cold. It's ruined now. You've wasted a whole cup of tea."

"You can't turn me away."

I kept my composure, refusing the fire that was ever ready to ignite in my chest. "If you won't drink my tea, I'm not sure the point of you staying here."

"Lily —"

"You can leave now."

"The Beast still hunts you, doesn't he?"

"It's harder for him to find me than it used to be."

"Right, sure," he said. "But that doesn't mean he can't. Just because you've covered your trail with all those poison medications you pour into yourself and just because you pay a fake doctor an ungodly amount of money to listen, and to sympathize, that doesn't mean that he isn't looking for you. He'll always be looking for you. What's the point in hiding like this? Nobody escapes him once he's got their scent. I've never understood why you won't simply surrender, save yourself some pain."

"You'd like that, wouldn't you?"

"I only want what's best for you, my sweet angel," he said.

I burst upright from my chair, sparks - though not fire - hit against the lining of my stomach. "I'm not an angel, and I sure as fuck am not yours."

He watched me for a moment, moving closer. "I am you, my darling. I own you."

My face burned. "No one owns me. Seraphina tried, but nobody can. Not even the Beast, and certainly not you."

He stroked my cheek. The cottony membrane of his soft skin was almost like elastic. I sucked in hard through my teeth, against the vile sensation of his caress. I ripped away from him, sneering.

"You have always been my dearest treasure. I've known many, I've owned many, but I've never had one as beautiful as you."

My hands sliced across his cheek, whipping against his white flesh. His head jerked to the side, but his broad smile refused to dissipate.

"Don't touch me."

He turned his gaze and head back to me, massaging the sore part of his face with his fingertips, still smiling. "Alone will always mean lonely for you. Always. But I'll never leave you, not really."

"You're nothing without me," I hissed. "You don't even exist unless I do. You're desperate for me to remember you, to know you, so you can go on living."

"You're a fool if you think you're the only know I come to."

I turned around, facing my stag head. "Why would you ask for tea if you weren't going to drink it?"

"It could be so much easier than this."

"It's my favorite flavor of tea and you just wasted it."

His breathing was staggered behind me, halting and shuddering. I thought I may have even heard a soft chuckle, but perhaps it was just the old cabin creaking. His approaching footsteps signaled his arrival behind me, and I felt as his hot breath moistened the back of my neck.

"You think you're a God," I said.

"Who are you to tell me that I am not? Think of the things I made you do. Think of how I controlled your brain, a puppet-master pulling strings. Tell me those weren't the actions of a God."

The silence settled in a heavy snowfall around us. His breath stopped blowing on my skin, and I felt him backing away. Without turning to look fully at him, I knew that his gaze remained on me. I knew how he always watched. I would not stare back. I was always thirty-seven years old. I would never again be twenty-one.

The door slammed. My knees weakened with relief at his departure. I looked back at the dead stag. I reached up and pressed my fingertips against the stag's ebony black nose.

"Do you think Pierre would have ever done this to Natasha?" I asked the stag.

He did not reply.

I looked down through the window and out into the night. It was so dark that I could not see the forest that lay just beyond the cabin. Not even a single owl hooted, no wolves howled. It was difficult to imagine that any world existed outside of the one housed in that cabin. My hand fell away from the stag. I opened the window. A cool breeze danced in and rushed in through the screen and against my face.

"You'll give in to me, sooner than you think," the voice said in my head.

"Shh, shh, shh. Not now, not right now."

"Why not?" he questioned, his voice echoed in through my skull. "You don't want the Beast to hear you talking to me? Think that'll make him find you quicker?"

"You're it's henchman, he owns you."

"How are you? Shut up, you have no right to say that to me," he cried, deafening me for a moment.

I winced, reaching over to clutch my braid. "No."

"What did you say?"

"No, I won't 'shut up,' I won't."

His laugh burned the inside of my head. "Why bother with it now? Despite what you may think, I never really left you. Not really, not completely."

I stared out into the darkness. Ichabod was out there somewhere. Ichabod survived. Ichabod lived. Ichabod was real.

"Yes."

"I know everything about you."

"Do you? What do you know?"

"I know your favorite composer."

"It's Stravinsky, that's not difficult."

"Still, I know it," he said.

I gripped my braid tighter, pulling against the follicles as they remained hooked onto my scalp. "What's my favorite song?"

"Excuse me?"

"You heard me."

He chuckled within my skull. "Your favorite song? 'The Firebird Suite', of course. Do you think I'm a fool?"

I felt myself awaken. My eyes adjusted to the dark. I could make out just a hint of a pine tree.

"I do love the finale, I love I way I danced to it, but that was never my favorite."

The voice went silent for a moment. "You're a fool to lie to me."

"Beethoven."

"No specifics?"

"Beethoven's 'Piano Concerto No. 5. Emperor.'"

"See? You cannot lie to your owner."

"In E-flat major. Op. 73."

I listened to the voice as it whispered in my brain, nearly incoherent until it murmured, "Liar."

My heart ached from palpitating so quickly. "I know how lonely you are."

"How could Freddie Mercury be your favorite? You always loved David Bowie."

"I used to love you because I was lonely, too."

"Your mind is my mind. I am embedded in you; as the blood that flows through your veins. You are nothing, you are nowhere. We've been together too long for your reality to exist in any other way."

"I love Beethoven's Emperor Piano Concerto No. 5."

"You'll never know true freedom."

"You don't understand freedom. I am free. I am not your prisoner."

"The Beast owns you. No matter what you say about me, he'll always own you."

"No one can own me."

"You're not a God, either, you know."

I stared out of the window. My eyes fixated on the one pine tree I could make out in the ebony night. I looked down at my stubby, bitten-down nails and pressed my clammy hands into the windowsill. My body swayed gently. I did not respond to the voice, and without any reply, the voice dissipated from my brain.

I looked back to Dandelion, and then to the decapitated stag. This cabin was a dead place, a lost place floating out somewhere in the cosmos. I would never run Seraphina's curls through my fingers again. I would never again watch wrinkles form around her honey brown eyes when she smiled. I would never again hear her sharp, high-pitched laughter. The wind was sucked out of my lungs, I bent down to rest my elbows on my knees, a whiteness gathered behind my eyes. My hands began to shiver, and then my body quaked violently out of control.

I staggered forward to the stuffed stag head. The pain burned into me as I clenched my jaw, sucking in air. I screamed. My voice bellowed through the cabin. It echoed across the empty woods and seeped into the decaying walls. I refused to break eye contact with the stag. I forced myself to see.

I eventually ran out of breath and dropped onto the musty floor. My lungs throbbed for want of air. My braid dangled over my shoulder. I would have died if I was to stay in that place, the rot would infect me. I put my hand to the ground, forcing myself upright before I was tempted to stay on the floor forever. This place would destroy me if I did not destroy it first.

I gathered remnants of memory in my pockets, taking the last of my money and little objects I did not want to be lost. I jolted as the phone rang again. My head snapped toward the brutal sound. I pressed the receiver to my ear and mouth.

"Who is this?" I said.

"Lily?"

"Sera?"

She breathed heavily. "God. I — I don't…how are you? Are you alright?"

I had never heard her distraught. My eyes flickered back and forth furiously. My lips moved closer to the phone.

"I'm at the cabin." Of course I was.

"I know. Have you seen it?"

I looked up to the stag, my jaw locked together. "Seen what?"

I heard her swallow. "You know what, Lily."

"I want you to say it."

I heard her shuffle on the other end of the line. "The taxidermized deer."

"Yes. I've seen it."

"I'm sorry, God, I'm so sorry. I shouldn't have put that thing up. I shouldn't have made you look at it. I shouldn't have shot the fucking thing in the first place."

I forced my breathing to remain steady. "But you did. You murdered it."

"Yes, Lily. I shot a deer," she said.

"You shot a *stag*, 'Phee."

She stammered for a while, her words halting after a few minutes. "I knew you were going to leave. God, I was so angry with you. I wanted to hurt you for not loving me anymore."

My voice rose and thickened as I snapped, "I adore you. I'll always adore you."

"Then why would you leave? Why didn't you even tell me you were going?"

"You killed a stag."

"Yes. I did."

I nodded slowly. "I love you."

"I love you. Lily, I'm sorry."

"Thank you. Thank you for loving me. Thank you for letting me love you."

"I shouldn't have killed the stag. I know that now."

"I'll find you again, one of these days."

"Lily —"

I hung up before she could finish. I began to hear the hesitant singing of early mourning doves. I wandered toward the window, chewing on my lower lip until it gushed blood.

A small piece of the sky beamed with soft, yellowish light; the sun has just begun to loom over the edge of the horizon. I blinked. A smile rose on my lips as tears began to trail down my cheeks. I turned and gazed back at the inside of the cabin. This building was a sore on this land, it blocked the sunlight.

Seraphina always kept a few gallons of gasoline in the lower cupboard. She always made sure the container was airtight and protected from the elements. She also stored a book of matches in what used to be our bedroom for lighting candles.

It took me a moment to open the gasoline. Once I do, I angled the container down, spilling the foul-smelling liquid onto the wooden floors, on the carpets, on the couch, sprinkling it on the furniture. When I finished with one container, I opened another, and then another. I took care to avoid Dandelion, keeping my plush swan dry. I picked up the phone for the third time that day and dialed the emergency station.

Before the dispatcher had time to question me, I said, "There's a fire up at Seraphina Ramsey's cabin. Do you know where that is?"

There was a short stammer on the other end of the line. "Did you say, 'a fire'?"

"Do you know where Seraphina's cabin is?"

"Seraphina Ramsey? Her cabin's on fire?"

"Yes. You need to get up here as fast as you can."

"Uh — sorry, I'm sorry, ma'am, but what is your name? Where are you? Are you safe? Is anyone inside?"

"No, the cabin's empty. Empty."

"What is your name, ma'am?"

My eyes flicked over to gaze out of the window. The sun had risen higher into the sky. I was running out of time.

"I was hiking in the woods, and I saw that there was a fire."

"Ma'am, I'm showing that you're calling from inside the house. I'm going to ask again; what is your name? Are you alright?"

"No. The cabin's empty." I pushed the phone back down without another word.

I felt raw, exhausted, yet vibrantly awake. I turned around and cradled the final, near-empty can of gasoline in the crook of my elbow. I cocked my head as I stared up at the stag.

"You're going to be free," I said. "I'll set you free."

I sprayed the last of the liquid onto the stag. Its fur dripped. My heart raced and my fingers trembled as I removed a match from its bed, allowing it to rest before my gaze. The Firebird taught me the power of the flame. Though, I had never truly utilized it before that moment. She whispered in my ear about the miracle of an inferno, but I was not listening. I had always thought of the blaze in me as destructive, but the Firebird was trying to tell me about the phoenix. New life, rebirth. We were all created in a moment of immense fire when God exploded the universe into existence all those many eons ago. Ashes and sparks from the burning stars fostered our evolution. Fire begets the dusty cinders that we will all be reduced to when the sun cremates the Earth into soot. The universe will die, just as every star must implode into a blazing supernova. God will end us all in a glorious inferno. We will all return to the ash that brought us into existence. In that place, I would be with my long-dead butterfly again, with the Blonde in the Pond, with Aurora, and that is where I would again find Seraphina.

I plucked Dandelion from the couch and tucked her underneath my arm. I used that same hand to hold the matchbook steady, swiping the match across the surface with as much vigor as my quivering fingers would allow. I gave birth to a tiny flame that would quickly blossom into a great blaze. I glanced up at the stag one last time. I tossed the match up, and within moments, it's fur caught flame. Its neck burned first, then the fire climbed up to its snout, engulfing its head. It did not take long for the blaze to move onto the wall and then down to the floor. I lit another match and threw it onto the stained carpet. I tossed another onto the floral couch. Without watching to see the fire's growth, I turned, going quickly from the cabin before I could see any longer. I turned as I walked backwards across the mossy grass. My shoes were so thin that I felt the softness of the ground below me.

I pressed Dandelion into my chest and stroked my hand over the swan's head as we watched the cabin build into a pyre. Sirens blared in the distance. I wondered how long I had been standing there. They were close enough now that they would be able to extinguish the flames before they could lick the tree branches or the dewy ground. I hugged Dandelion. I then took off in a sprint in the opposite direction and through the woods. I knew a shortcut to the village from there. There was a train station that led to the next town where I would find an airport. I would be gone before anyone could see me.

My eye caught a glimpse of something, stalling my feet in their flight. Two gleaming yellow eyes stared at me from under the brush. I halted, smiling at Ichabod as he watched me go. Before I could reach out to touch him, he sauntered away in the opposite direction. His coal-colored fur mingled with the last of the night's blackness as the sun continued to float upward. The sunrise was painted with golds and whites and hints of pink. My chilled skin began to tingle with hints of warmth as I went through the woods. The doves continued to sing, blissfully unaware of my presence. The cabin was transformed into ash.

Chapter 8
The Present, Light

Lily watched as Aurora flipped through her copy of *War and Peace*. Her mind was mixed and muddled. The only thing that was clear was Seraphina's curls as the wind danced with them and the soft warmth of her lips. Aurora noticed her staring.

"Are you alright?" She allowed the novel to rest on her stomach.

"Yes, sorry. Distracted."

Aurora nodded. "Did you have a session with The Doctor today?"

"Yes."

"How did that go?"

"So stupid. It was a massive waste of time. You know about him. You know how he is."

She sat up straighter in bed. "No, actually. He's never treated me."

Lily furrowed her brow. "What? Why?"

Aurora shrugged. "He just never has. I think I scare him. He barely even looks at me."

"How long have you been here?"

"Too long. Years. It feels like I've been here since forever. My family dropped me off here and never looked back; my mother never really knew what to do with me."

Lily was uncomfortable with the sensitivity rising in the room. "My sister is the same. I confuse her."

Aurora looked over Lily's shoulder and out into the stark darkness. Lily had not even realized that night had fallen.

"I wish I could go outside, even for a walk," Aurora signed.

"You can. We can leave whenever we want to."

"Not me. They think I'll kill myself the moment I step foot outside."

Lily smirked. "Why would they think that?"

"Because I tried to the last time."

Lily's lips pursed, the grin vanishing from her lips. "Sorry. It isn't any of my business."

Aurora's eyes lost some of their fog and she waved her off. "No. I'm not used to talking about it. Did I make you uncomfortable?"

"Of course not. I…" She could not finish her sentence.

"I did, I know it. I always do, I always make people uncomfortable, especially when I talk about what I tried to do."

Lily swallowed, all at once desperate for something to say. "What happened?"

Aurora paused before replying, "It's hard to remember. I know that I was out in the woods, and everything was dead. I thought that everything in the world had died, and I was the only one left alive. I remember how the rope felt in my hand. It was hard to tie it over the tree branch. It made a rash burn on my left palm. It caught some of my hair when I put my neck through it, and I remember falling. And then…" Aurora's hands stopped. They dropped to hang limply by her waist. "Sometimes I wonder why I still have to be here. How could the rope be any worse than this?"

Lily's eyes watered, she blinked rapidly. "I understand."

"I never stop being tired, I never stop being stuck. My neck is still in that rope. I can hardly breathe. And nobody knows or sees me."

"I know," Lily signed. "I can still feel the bathwater on my skin, always."

Aurora folded her legs up onto her bed. She seemed to fall back into herself, collapsing like a deer as a bullet careens into its side.

"No, sorry. I need to sleep."

Aurora threw herself down onto the mattress, flinging the covers over her head.

Lily tilted her head back slightly, taken aback by the abrupt change. She remained upright, watching her figure breathe rapidly beneath the comforter. Then Lily backed up slowly back onto her bed. She slid herself beneath the covers, her bones and limbs creaked. Her hair buried her in long strands, she wanted to push it back, but restrained herself. She did not wish to disturb Aurora. Lily pressed the side of her head deeper into the pillow. The silence became muffled as her ear was entombed. In the cold quiet, her mind drifted away from her. She was taken into an unsettled slumber.

The next time she felt consciousness, there was a glowing light that shone just beyond her eyelids. Lily took a hard breath in, squinting and rubbing the back of her hand across her forehead. She had never felt the sun like that before. The color yellow was all too bright and too soft. She propped herself up on her elbow and looked towards Aurora's bed. She was still asleep. A spider spun a knotted web in the pit of her stomach, and she felt all at once nauseous and ill. It did not feel like daytime, it did not feel like morning. She knew that the moon was shining on the back of her head. She spun herself around, her palms falling to lie flat on the bed. She craned her neck back and pulling her hand up to shield her eyes from the light, which presented itself as a massive orb hovering before her window. It was not the sun.

The light burned her corneas. Her head felt as though it had been set aflame; she wanted to feel her hair to make sure it wasn't blazing. Yet, before she could, a sharp pinch in her belly pulled her upward. Her pelvis levitated above her head and drew her toward the ceiling. She felt disorientated. The further she traveled up, the less aware she became.

It was not long before her entire body was hovering in mid-air, and she began to travel toward the window. Her hair spread through the invisible air as though she was submerged underwater. Her figure moved through the window and out into the frigid night. She knew that it was cold. She was aware of the snow, yet she could not feel it against her skin. The stars were obscured by ice-filled clouds, though the flurries kept her from seeing them clearly. She continued to drift until she flew into an open door. She entered the light, until, finally, the pull in her stomach and pelvis gave way. She toppled downward, slamming onto a cold floor.

She sat up, gasping, and throwing her arms out to her sides to steady herself. Her palms were flat against the hard ground. She looked to the side and saw a group of them, one was off to the right on its own, five others were huddled closely together. They looked as though they had just emerged from an ancient ocean, as though they ought to be long-extinct; or perhaps as if they never should have existed at all. Lily's body began to shake out of control, and a scream ripped through her throat. The ear-piercing sound rippled in echoes throughout the orb she was trapped in, but the beings did not startle. She scrambled back until she hit the curved wall.

"Jesus," she called out, gathering her knees up to her chest and wrapping her arms around them.

After a moment, the isolated creature suddenly made a deep hum, like the low, penetrating song of a whale. The force of the cry hurt her ears, and she slammed her palms over them. The other five joined in, and there arose a chorus of their strange voices, a choir that appeared to be harmonizing with each other. They floated toward her, loosely hovering above the silver floor. She did not move. Every portion of her body felt brittle, frail. But they kept coming until they were inches away from her. Then, they rose in unison. They wormed upward until they nestled themselves in her hair. She grimaced, her lips quivering, but she did nothing to try and escape. The beings latched onto her scalp like a leech against skin, stinging lightly.

They grew fluorescent with color, their bodies glowing as the gleaming light which ballooned in their bodies and traveled down them. All at once, Lily's body jolted, as if she had been shocked, though she did not feel any pain. Her head snapped back, and her eyes clouded over with white webbing.

She was lifted upward once more, then dropped back down. Euphoria and dopamine flooded her bloodstream. She felt the sensation of movement, and the silver walls became translucent. She rushed through blackness, stars, and planets. She knew that she was alive, but she could not feel any fragment of her body. She only knew the surge of speed as she went, along with the light which transmitted through the strange bodies and into her. For a few moments, she was nothing and everything at once. She felt each particle of the universe as though it passed through her, each atom. She felt the chaos and connection that bound the cosmos, and she felt a presence. She felt a force. She felt something that spun everything together in a fabric. It was loose, watery, but it was there.

She was unsure if hours passed or merely minutes, but the movement finally slowed. The darkness moving past her stalled, the creatures simultaneously disconnecting themselves from her scalp. Weakness took her over, and her back arched and drooped. She crashed into the floor before looking back up. The creatures had not moved, save for allowing themselves to dangle beneath beside her. She reached out to them, her fingers quivering.

"Come back," she whispered.

They did not move toward her, but instead drifted apart, forming a circle around her. Her legs turned cold. The ground beneath her was thinning.

"Please don't leave."

The floor disintegrated in its entirety. She fell through, rushing down into a deep abyss that tunneled her into nothingness. She dropped into liquid, yet she could still breathe. She put her arm out, her fingers bent into a claw as she ran her hands through the emptiness before her. Never had she heard such complete silence. The further she floated, the more light she could see. She tipped her head down, a glow meeting her eyes. The odd creatures from the craft drifted down along with her. She watched as their bodies slowly began to break apart, splintering into tiny orbs. They traveled faster than her, and she watched as they passed her by.

She might have been there for eons.

Before long, the orbs multiplied, and the glow expanded through the blue gel. She saw millions of spheres, yellow and gleaming. They formed a swirling circle around her in a gradual vortex. She reached out and pushed back again, propelling herself forward. She grasped one of the luminous balls in her palm. It was spongy and molded to the shape of her hand. All at once, the same deep moans radiated from the orbs. Their whale-like cries seeped into her brain. The low hum spoke to her, and she understood. She cracked her lips open, pressing the sphere into her mouth. Her teeth mashed down, but it slipped down and onto her tongue. Her eyes widened, and she fought the urge to spit it out. The whale song started up again, and she forced the orb to stay in her mouth. She bent her head back and pressed her tongue down into the depth of her throat until it slid down. She gasped, and the glare intensified. Light shone until there was nothing.

Stars were born and died inside of her stomach. Supernova.

When the light finally faded and drained away, her eyes were flushed with darkness. She saw that the heavens had cleared. The swirls of silver clouds had dissipated. Tiny droplets of light sparkled in the velvet black. She was horizontal and floated to the left. She wanted to look to the side to see if the ship was still visible, but the muscles in her neck would not allow it. A few moments later, she passed through the frame of her window. The stars were shielded from her by the popcorn bubbled white ceiling. The yellow light's fingers grazed against her face one last time. Then, it dripped out of the room, and she gently came to rest down on the cushion of her bed.

She gasped again, her chest heaving as she flung herself up. The silvery metallic craft was gone. She only knew that she was breathing. There was a rapping against the bed beside her, and Lily turned to see Aurora sitting straight up in bed. The moonlit made her face glow. She lifted her hands up.

"What was it like?" she signed.

Lily put her arms up to her chest. Her fingers twitched to tell her what had happened.

"It was…" she began, but she dropped her hands back into her lap. She laid down. Her hair splayed over the pillow, thick and heavy.

***

Lily had been instructed to wait for group therapy in the common room. Nurse Kathy told her to 'relax and watch the T.V.' *The Wizard of Oz*, 1939, was playing on the platformed television. Lily's hair was roped back in a French braid, her bangs falling over her right eyebrow. She rubbed her bare arms to suppress the goosebumps. She felt naked without her sweater. She smiled when she saw Poe reading in his usual chair.

"What are you reading?" she asked.

"*We Have Always Lived in the Castle*. Shirley Jackson. Don't tell anyone though, I think they'd take it away if they knew. Just trying to put my brain to some use before it enters the final stages of decomp," he said. "You look pretty."

Why should she care if he called her pretty? She tried to swallow the warmth in her face. "I'm tired of having hair in my face all the time. And I needed to wash my sweater."

"Why not just cut it?"

"No. I can't do that."

"Why?"

"Because I can't. Everyone tells me I shouldn't."

"What does that matter?"

"I don't know."

"Do you like it?"

"No," she snapped. She surprised herself with the force of her reply.

He stared at her for a moment, then looked back down to his book. "There you are, then."

She tugged on her braid again.

"Lily. My, you look so pretty this morning," The Doctor's voice called out from a distance.

Her stomach filled with sickness.

"Aren't you cold?" he asked.

"I'm fine."

"Hmm," he said. "Well, Poe, Lily, are you ready for group? I have a feeling this will be a fruitful session."

"Oh, Christ," Poe hissed under his breath.

She was unsure if The Doctor had heard him. "Shall we go? The rest of the group is waiting."

"Well, fuck, then," Poe whispered to her.

Poe and Lily stood from their seated positions and followed behind The Doctor. As the three of them rounded the corner, a pod of people sat in a circle and flipped their gazes toward them.

"I'd like to keep this session informal," The Doctor announced to the group. He sat down in his seat. His metal chair clanged with the motion.

The session began as it often did. It did not take long for Lily's mind to drift.

"Lily?" The Doctor said.

"Yes?"

"What are you thinking about?"

"What?"

"Tell us what you're thinking about right now. Give us a glimpse into that mind of yours," he said.

She looked down at her hair. It was dead and split at the ends. "I'm not thinking about anything," she said.

"Come now, we all know that isn't the case. Just say the first thing that comes to your head, right now."

Her thoughts were twisted and distorted as she scoured it for something to say.

"The Golden Record," she finally said in a rush, unsure how the words felt on her tongue.

"I beg your pardon?"

"The Golden Record, on the Voyager. I guess. I don't know."

"Oh, alright. Well, go on."

She shrugged and stared down at the tiled floor. She scrubbed a mark of grime off the ground with the heel of her shoe. "Nothing. I just like the idea of it."

"The idea of what?"

"The Voyagers were supposed to be out in space for two years. But they're just going to keep going, forever, or for as long as we understand forever to be. I like that."

"You've always had this interest in space?" The Doctor asked.

Lily still refused to look up at him. "Yeah, I guess. When I was little, I thought that there was a whale that lived underneath the ice layer on Europa."

She finally looked up. Her chest burned as the rest of the group stared at her. She had unsettled them. She hunched her back, her bangs flopped over her eye.

"Well, thank you, dear. That was very interesting, wasn't it? Have you ever considered that your preoccupation with space, and the

Golden Record, may have something to do with the reason you're here today?"

"No, not really."

"The cosmos are chaotic, out of our control. Do you think perhaps your struggle with your temper has to do with a lack of control? Just as space is wild and confusing, so are your outbursts. Would you say that's true? Perhaps you relate yourself to it in that way."

"No, I don't have… When I danced, I could control it."

"But you haven't danced in quite some time, isn't that right?"

"No, but I —"

"So, in truth then, you have no way to control yourself now?"

"Why won't you let me finish talking? You always talk over me."

"I'm simply trying to understand. I want you to trust me, to trust us."

"Dance was my only way to —"

"This is a safe place."

"Yes, I know. But I -"

"You can talk to everyone here."

"Please stop it."

"This is a process, you know."

"Stop it."

"Lily, you're never going to get any better until you admit you have a problem."

She leapt up, and, without warning, reached back to grab the frame of her chair. She thrust it over her head. It went hurtling toward The Doctor then clattered to the ground with a crash.

"Why don't you listen to me?" she screamed. "If she'd left me in the bathtub then none of this would have happened!"

The Doctor looked down at the fallen chair. He sighed. "Really, dear."

Her furious panting filled the room. She looked down at the

destroyed chair. She threw her hand over her mouth. Her eyes fell over to Poe, who had the side of his head and temple dropped into his hand. Her bottom lip began to quiver, and she shrank into herself. She thought that last night had proven that she could be different.

"I'm sorry. I don't want to be like this, this way. It's him, he makes me the way I am." Her voice became murky.

Poe reached out and put his fingertips against her bare arm. "Lily."

The Doctor reached down and pulled the chair from the ground. He folded what was left of the metal chair back out, moving past her to place it in the empty space where it had been before. It was bent. It was not quite broken enough to collapse if someone sat in it, but it would never truly sit flat again.

"Go ahead and sit back down. Angela, would you like to share next?"

Lily could not recall the remainder of the session, and was only aware of Poe's fingertips as they remained rested against her arms.

She awakened only when she laid over the comforter of the bed, her arms wrapped over her stomach and her ear pressed into the pillow.

"I hate Natasha," Aurora signed, not removing her eyes from the novel that rested in her lap.

Lily had one hand tucked underneath her temple as she laid on her side at the edge of the bed. She gave her a small chuckle, despite her exhaustion.

She pulled her hands out, signing, "How was your day?"

"Boring. You?" Aurora signed.

"Not great. My fault, though."

"Too bad."

Lily sat up. She glanced out the window at the white snow swirling outside. "It's almost Christmas, right?"

"Is it?"

"I think so. It's hard to tell, I don't know how long I've been here. It feels like I've been here forever, other times it feels like a day or two.

I don't think my family will come to see me for Christmas, the Doctor said I'd be home by now."

Aurora turned her head to the wall. "The Doctor lies. Neither of us are ever getting out of here."

***

"I've never liked Christmas," Poe said. "Never a great time for me."

Lily stared up at the showing of *The Wizard of Oz* and put her palm in the middle of her chest where her four-way cross used to hang. "I love Christmas. Mass was always prettiest on Christmas."

"You're Catholic?"

"Used to be," she said. "This'll be the first year I miss mass on Christmas."

"Just tell The Doctor you want to go out to church. He'll let you. Much as they make you think otherwise, we're not actually in a prison here."

"I guess."

"What's wrong?"

She pressed her damp hands together, putting them between the sweatpants on her thighs. Her shirt for that day was boxy with a collar and sky-color hue. She was still not wearing her chenille sweater. Her hair was secured to the back of her head in a braided bun.

"Nothing. I don't really want to talk about it." She pulled her knees up to her chest. "I'm sorry. I'm just tired."

Lily's mind consumed the small clips of noises that filtered in from around the room all at once. Books folded and opened, little voices chippered about the space, and Dorothy discovered the true meaning of home.

"My family hasn't even called," she said. "I feel like they've forgotten about me."

"You and me, both," Poe said.

Finally, she tore her eyes from the television screen and to him. "Shepard really won't come? Even to visit?"

Poe's eyes grew red. "No. He won't. I think I've been forgotten, too."

Lily was all at once filled with the desire to run her fingers through his hair and press their bodies together. But she did not.

"Lily?" The Doctor's voice called. "You have a visitor, dear."

She spun around in her chair. "What?"

"Your sister is waiting in the lobby."

Poe offered her a little smile.

"Why is she here?" Lily asked, standing and rushing ahead of The Doctor. The heels of her old sneakers smacked against the ground as they neared the lobby.

"She wants to see you, I imagine," he said. "It's almost Christmas, you know."

Maggie was perched in one of the blue, oddly formed plastic chairs. Her thumbs were pressing into her phone. Her brown hair was fastened back in a ponytail. Lily's teeth melded together. Her hands rolled up into a fist. Her nails pressed deeply into her skin.

"Maggie?" she asked softly.

Her sister broke her gaze from her phone. "Hey, sweetie. Good to see you."

"What are you doing here?" Lily said.

"It's Christmas, isn't it? I just wanted to see how you're getting along. Sit down with me for a minute."

Lily reached for another of the egg-shaped blue chairs without looking. "Where are mom and dad? Did they come?"

"No. You know how busy they are, and they've never liked things like this."

Lily relaxed slightly. "Right. Yeah, I know."

Maggie cleared her throat and signaled for The Doctor to leave them alone. After he left, Maggie folded her arms against the table. "No sweater. Hard to believe they've done what I've been trying to do for over a year now. See how pretty you can be if you actually try?"

"It's hot in here, they never turn on the air conditioning."

"It's snowing outside. Would you rather be out there?"

"No."

"Then there's no good in complaining."

"I wasn't."

"I wanted to give you a compliment, why can't you just say thank you?"

"Sorry."

Maggie scoffed. "Okay, sure. I'm sorry, I don't want to upset you. I'm not trying to start a fight."

Lily wanted to stand up and burst through the window and run off into the woods. She wanted to leave her shoes behind and feel the grass and dirt against her scarred, bent feet. She wanted to travel so far away that Maggie would never see her again. The skin would melt away from her skeleton, and the Earth would eat her, devour her. She would be in the roots of the trees, and one day a stag's hooves might pass over her corpse, and he'd know that she was there.

"I'm getting fat here. All I do is eat and sleep," Lily whispered.

Maggie sucked in a gulp of air. "I see you're still saying that. I mean, you know you aren't fat. You know that."

"I didn't use to be."

"I like your hair like that, you look so much older," Maggie said.

"I was thinking about cutting it."

"What?" Maggie said. "Do you know how many people would kill to have hair like yours? Mom would never forgive you."

"It was just an idea."

"You'd better not. Don't be stupid."

"Okay."

Maggie reached down to grab a bag glittered with red sparkles and painted with the image of golden Christmas bells. Green wrapping paper fluttered out of the top.

"I'd better get to the reason I came before we get into a real fight."

"What is that?"

"Your Christmas present. Obviously, we were all hoping you'd be back home by now, but it doesn't look like that going to happen. We're going to stay at the MacLaine's house, you remember them? Chris and Rachel? It's been a long time since we've seen their baby. We're leaving tonight.

Lily's throat throbbed. Was it truly so easy to live without her?

"Go on, open it. Kathy and your doctor already approved it."

Lily placed the gift onto her lap. She saw a white, fluffy creature poke its head out from the depths of the wrapping paper. She yanked it out by its neck. In her hands she held a plush swan, only a few inches tall with a stuffed body. It had plastic blue eyes.

"What is this?" She twisted it around in her hands.

"It's a swan," Maggie said, her voice squealing with excitement.

"Yeah. No, I know, but why?"

"I thought it was cute, it reminded me of when you were in *Swan Lake.*"

"When my Achilles Tendon snapped?"

Maggie's eyes flashed to the side. Her chest rose and fell unevenly. Lily knew her sister wanted The Doctor to come back.

"Is that when that happened? I'd forgotten."

"Yeah."

"It reminded me of you, that's all. I thought you'd like it."

Lily put her palm on its feathers. The blue eyes stared back at her. She had nothing in common with this creature. How was it that her own sister thought of her short time as an understudy for Odette and Odile, neither of whom she played, while obliterating the memory of the initial ruination of her body? She had always felt that her role as the leftmost dancer in the Four Little Swan variation was her most unimpressive.

She smiled a little. "Thanks, it's cute."

Maggie sighed loudly. "Oh, good. Great. You're welcome."

Lily pressed the plush swan into her chest, its firm beak pushed into her shirt. "It reminds me of Odette. Post-Rothbart's spell, I guess."

Maggie clapped her hands together. "I knew you'd love it."

"I'm sorry I didn't get you and mom and dad anything."

She waved her off. "No, no. Don't worry about that."

"Have fun at the MacLaine's. Tell them I said 'hi', but I'm not sure they remember me."

"Of course they do, and I will. I'll try to give you a call Christmas morning. But you know how forgetful I am."

Lily bit down onto her cheek until pain shot through her jaw, forcing her smile to remain fixed to her lips. "Yeah, I know."

Maggie pressed her phone until it flashed to life. "I've got to run. Jud is coming over to the house and we need to collect the eggs from the henhouse before we leave."

"I know. It's okay," she replied.

Maggie smiled as she rose from the chair. She put her palm over Lily's knuckles for a moment.

"Take care, sweetie. You look so much better already."

She did not wait for Lily to respond. Instead, she threw her phone in her purse and spun on her heels, her ponytail twirled behind her shoulders. She went down the beige hall and through the glass doors. Lily was left holding the swan on her lap.

"What a cute toy, dear," The Doctor said.

"Thanks."

"Would you like to put it on your bed?"

"No. I want to go to the common room."

"With the stuffed animal?"

"Yeah." She stood up. She cradled the swan within her arm and walked ahead of The Doctor. Something in her was all at once liberated, free. She stroked her sweaty palm over the swan's feathery wing. Suddenly, she was desperate to see Seraphina.

"When is my next ride?" she asked.

"Pardon?"

"When is Seraphina coming back?"

"She won't be coming for Christmas."

"But she's Wiccan," Lily said.

"Still, we're not allowing any riders to come this week. She'll be here the day after."

"She can't come any sooner?"

"Afraid not. She lives up on the mountain, she's not the easiest to get ahold of. Though I am so glad that you want to see her. It's always nice when a friendship forms between teacher and student."

They entered the common room and Lily rushed back toward the seat parallel to where Poe was still sitting. She did not allow her eyes to turn back but heard The Doctor's footsteps fade away into the tentative general noises that surrounded them. She sat down next to Poe and folded her hands over the swan in her lap.

He looked up at her, his gaze fixed on the swan, then back to his book. "Hey. How was that?"

"Pretty good."

"Still want to go out on Christmas?"

"I don't want to go to mass."

"You don't have to."

"They won't just let us leave. I know you think they will, but it won't happen," Lily said.

He glanced at her from the side; he really was beautiful. "I used to be Catholic, too. I mentioned it once in group, so The Doctor will know I'm not lying. We could ask to be driven to church by Nurse

Kathy, or anyone, I suppose it doesn't matter. We tell them to pick us up after the service, but we could sneak away once they've driven off. We just have to make sure to be back at the front of the church when they roll by to pick us up."

"They'd never leave us alone."

"Kathy would, if we pushed her on it."

She sat silent for a moment, one of the moths that lived in her brain traveled down her throat and into her stomach, fluttering there against the lining of her belly. "Do you really think so?"

"Sure, why not? It'd be nice to get some fresh air, really fresh. And not everything is closed on Christmas, I know we could find something to do."

She could not recall the last time anyone had the desire to spend any more time with her than was necessary. "Let's ask her today, so she has time and we don't spring it on her. It'll look less suspicious if we do it that way."

"You make it sound so dramatic. We aren't pulling off a heist, we're only going out and not telling the whole truth about it."

"We're lying, it's pretty different." She stroked the swan's head.

"I can't tell if you're excited or dreading it," he said. Then he smiled. "You're sweet. I wish I was sweet like you."

The luscious, almost unbearable feeling in her gut soured. She dug her nails into the swan's plush body.

Chapter 9
The Present, Jailbreak

"I just love Jesus," Poe said to Nurse Kathy from the backseat. "What a guy, you know?"

Lily rolled her eyes in her place directly next to him. She knew that he was trying to make her laugh.

"Well," Nurse Kathy replied, her voice strained and tight. "It's always comforting to believe in something."

"Absolutely, and thank you for doing this," he said. He leaned forward.

"Yeah, thanks," Lily added, hating the high pitch of her voice.

"Of course. We at Meadowlark never want to decrease the quality of life for our patients, do we?" she said.

Poe laughed too loudly along with her and elbowed Lily in the side.

"No, definitely not," he said.

"Now, remember, The Doctor wants you both back the moment mass is over," Nurse Kathy said.

"Naturally," Poe said.

"I'll pick you two up where I'll drop you off. Yes?"

"Yes, ma'am."

"Try not to dawdle, yes?"

"Of course, ma'am."

"We're having a group session early tomorrow, so we wouldn't want you to be too tired."

"Never, ma'am."

Lily angled her swan so its eyes gazed out of the window. She ran her fingers over its back and heard Nurse Kathy sign from the front of the car.

"Lily, don't you want to leave your swan in the car with me? I swear I'll take it right back to the room the moment I get back."

"No."

"The Doctor and I are both worried that this might be a step backward."

Lily pressed the swan into her stomach. "I'm fine."

"We'll discuss it tomorrow."

"You won't take it away from me."

"Excuse me?"

"Nothing."

Nurse Kathy's gaze cut into the rearview mirror. Lily's head bent down. Her hair collapsed over her shoulders. She was suffocating. She twisted her wrist behind her and gathered her hair into a ponytail. Then she breathed out, her eyes closed as air flushed against the back of her neck.

"Are we almost there?" she asked.

"We are, yes."

Lily's eyes did not open until the car made a turn and slowed. She released the hair from her grip and felt it as it draped against her back in a wave.

"Alright, here we are. This was the closest Catholic church I could find. I'd told them that you were coming, so you'll be able to get Communion."

"Very considerate of you," Poe said.

Lily moved her face to the window. Her temple knocked against the cold glass.

"I wish you'd have worn a coat, Lily. That sweater is very cute, but I don't think you'll be warm enough."

Lily placed her twitching fingers against the door handle. She bounced her leg. The vibration made her calf burn.

Nurse Kathy pulled up alongside the curb of the church. "I'll be here waiting for you, alright? Come outside right after the service ends."

"You have our word, ma'am."

Nurse Kathy twisted her body around in her seat. "Alright, then. Go on. Have a great time and I'll see you soon."

Lily all at once was penetrated with guilt. It pierced through her soul with a shard of ice.

"See you soon, ma'am."

"See you soon, kids."

Lily popped the door open to step out. Poe followed closely behind.

Her eyes drifted up to the red brick church. People smiled at her as they passed. She recognized that grin, a comfortable joy laced with stupor. She looked down and clutched her swan.

The morning of her Confirmation, terror had forced bile from her stomach and given her a monstrous migraine. She still remembered looking up at the massive, white, marble crucifix. For the first time in her life, she had felt a presence within her. The stone eyes of Christ had gazed down at her, and she smiled back. She heard the sweet nectar of His voice as it coated her soul. As she stood like a statue and gazed at Him, her mother had clasped her fingers around her upper arm, her red fingernails had pressed into her flesh.

"What's wrong with you?" she had said. "Why did you stop? You're embarrassing me."

Lily clicked her two canine teeth together. She felt dirty, filthy even, standing at the foot of the church. She could very nearly see the thin pane of glass that separated her from Him. She wondered who had put it there.

"Wave until she's gone," Poe whispered to her. "We don't want to look suspicious."

"And you said this wasn't anything dramatic."

"It's not. But we're almost out. Wouldn't want to be shot by the guards on our way over the gate."

"Good Lord," she said.

Nurse Kathy's car disappeared out of sight.

"Thank you, Christ. For once, you really came through."

Lily's chest clenched. "Poe."

"Have you ever tried edibles?"

"What?"

"Weed. The THC level isn't that high."

"No."

"Would you like to try some?"

She narrowed her eyes and examined his face for a moment. "You don't actually have anything."

Poe pulled a plastic bag from his jacket, flashing a bundle of green-tinted candies. "There's nothing Nurse Calvin loves more than money."

Her mouth pried open. "Shit, Poe. What if we get arrested?"

He chuckled through his nose. "Don't be silly. We can always claim insanity in court."

"My dad would end my life if I ever got caught," she said as she overlaid her arms across her stomach.

"You can't live for your parents. It'll crush you in the end. If you want to give it a try, then try it."

She slowed down and watched her sneakers as they padded against the sidewalk. "It's not very strong?"

"No, not at all. Fucking infants could do this. I was a regular smoker before I came here. It makes you feel relaxed, that's all."

Lily felt the eyes of the church as they bored into the back of her skull. "I've never done anything. I only drank wine for Communion."

"This is great for a first-timer. You might not feel anything at all."

Her heart quickened its pace. It clawed against the bounds of her ribcage. "Give me one."

He dropped a gummy in her hand before pushing one into his mouth. Sugar stuck to her sweaty fingers as she examined the candy, saliva pooled on her tongue. She flung her palm up to her lips. She bit down before she could consider it. Bitterness flooded her mouth, and within an instant, slithered down her throat.

***

"I'm having a stroke."

"No."

"I'm having a heart attack."

"No."

"Holy shit, I need to need to go to the hospital."

"No."

"I can't breathe."

"You're hyperventilating. If you calm down —"

"Oh God, my fucking heart just stopped. Jesus Christ."

"I don't think so."

Lily cringed against her throbbing headache, fisting her fingers in her hair. "What the fuck is happening to me?"

"You're having a bad trip, I think."

"No."

"Yeah."

"I'm dying. I'm fucking dying."

"Honestly, I don't feel great either. Clearly not as bad as you, though," Poe slurred. "I think they were laced with something."

"Oh, God." she cried.

Poe threw his head back. "Stop, someone is going to call the police."

"I'm having a stroke. I can't even talk right."

"It'll wear off. I promise, you just need to ride it out."

"Fuck you."

"Okay."

She grasped the sleeve of his jacket limply. "You're trying to poison me."

"No."

"Then call an ambulance."

He pulled himself out of her grip. "Lily, stop. I feel like shit, too."

"I'm going to die of a weed overdose."

Poe ran his fingers through his hair. "It'll pass faster if you're distracted. Do you want to go and…I don't know…is there something you'd like to do?"

"I'm going to vomit."

"What?"

"I'm going to fucking puke."

"Oh, Christ."

Lily sprinted over to a black, grungy trash can, littered with bird feces and ripened with the scent of rotted food. She gripped the swan between her thighs. It's beak nearly dripped onto the garage bin. Bile thrashed around her stomach, and she waited for it to spew from her mouth. She felt Poe's hand as he twisted her hair back, holding it behind her ears.

"It'll happen, I'm going to barf," she said.

"That's fine, you'll probably feel better if you do."

They waited for what felt like eons. Nothing emerged from Lily's gut.

"It's not happening. What the fuck?" Lily said.

Poe released her hair. It fell heavy in a slap against her back.

"Just nausea, don't worry about it. It'll pass after a little while, just like everything else. I keep telling you."

She leaned back. Her hands were sticky from the garbage bin as she placed them on her hips. Her hair pulled against the skin on her skull and she gritted her teeth together.

"I hate my fucking hair. I fucking hate it. God, I just want to rip it off."

Poe threw his hands up. "You're screaming again!"

Lily slammed one fist into his arm. "So are you."

"Fuck you."

"Fuck you, you bastard. You've killed me."

He wobbled on his heels. "You're killing me. Jesus, you're a nightmare."

She breathed heavily through her nose, mashing her back teeth together. Every moment felt as though tiny faeries were dragging down each strand of hair, pulling against it, yet not quite hard enough to break the hair away from her skull.

"I can't stand it anymore," she said.

"Every trip ends, and you'll probably forget most of it anyway. By tomorrow you won't feel any of this."

"I want it off. Do you think any salons will be open?"

Poe bent his head. "I don't think that's a good idea. You always regret the stuff you do when you're fucked up."

"Can you find one that's open?"

He shakily retrieved his phone from his back pocket and typed in letters and numbers with significant effort. He scrolled down with his thumb as white light shone on his face. "Found one, *Discount Princess*."

"Get walking directions."

"This is a God-awful idea."

"Which direction?" Lily stumbled off toward nowhere in particular.

"You'll blame me for this tomorrow," he said. "We'll turn right at this next intersection."

***

"That's a significant cut, you sure that's how you want to do it?" the hairstylist asked. Her dyed blue hair slicked down against her neck with gel. She reeked of body odor and alcohol.

"Yeah, I'm sure," Lily said.

"If I were you, honey, I'd have to have a gun to my head before I got rid of any of it."

"Can you dye it? Maybe pink, or white. I think white would look cool."

"No, Lily," Poe shouted from his place on a ratty couch.

"Fuck off, you can't tell me what to do." Lily shot him a look through the mirror.

"Quit shouting, or you'll both be out of here." The blue-haired woman lifted her arm and allowed more of the pungent smell of her body to leak out.

"I really want curly hair, always have. Is there any way you could do that?" Lily pet the swan as it sat on her lap while she was perched on the scratched-up leather chair.

"You just could use a curling iron and hairspray."

"I want something more permanent than that."

The blue-haired woman's shoulders bunched up in frustration. "There are treatments, most don't work on hair as straight as yours."

"I don't need spirals or anything fancy."

"I guess we could always perm it."

"Yeah, yup. Perfect."

"Lily," Poe called. "What are you doing?"

"Nothing." She said. "How long will it take?"

"A little while. Are you sure about this? With a perm and that sweater, you'll look like you crawled right out of the 80s."

"I'll pay you."

"Of course you will."

"Then do it."

"It'll kill your hair, and it's so undamaged right now."

"Cut it first, obviously."

The blue-haired woman cocked one eyebrow as she stared at her reflection in the mirror. "Okay, fine. But don't blame me when you don't like the way it looks."

Lily's fingers wrapped around the swan's neck. "Show me the hair once it's cut. I want to see it."

Lily felt the pressure of the woman's scissors as they sliced across her hair, pulling at it. "Stay still. This is just the initial cut; I'll even it out afterwards."

Weight slowly slid away from her skull until it was freed from her entirely. So quickly, it all happened in the span of a few moments. A lifetime of weight evaporated like water on scolding concrete. A puff of air drifted out of her mouth, and she gasped quietly.

She heard Poe shift in his place on the couch. "Oh, God, Lily."

The stylist held up what looked like a horse's tail in her left hand. "Okay, you've seen it."

Tears flooded Lily's eyes, and she clamped her palm over her lips to keep the sobs from becoming audible.

"I told you not to blame me."

She waved her off.

"Thank you," she wept. "Thank you." Lily sucked a wad of saliva and mucus down her throat. "Okay, can we get on with the perm now?"

***

"I've always wanted to try champagne," Lily said.

She stumbled over her feet as her hair drifted up through the wind, bundled up in wadded, fluffy puffs.

"The last thing you need right now is alcohol."

"Champagne is hardly alcohol, and I'm feeling better now anyway."

Poe took a drag from his cigarette. The white excess air smelled foul as it hit her face and she inhaled the second-hand smoke. "You keep going through these spells, you have been for the past hour. You feel better and then you get paranoid and start panicking and acting crazy. You keep screaming about some animal that's after you, and then you're fine again. Honest to Christ, you don't need to be drunk right now."

"You can't tell me what to do."

He blew the smoke through his nostrils like a dragon. "I think the high is starting to wear off. Just wait a little while longer, I think we're through the worst of it."

"Nurse Kathy is going to end our lives, you know." Lily stroked her loose curls.

"Who's Nurse Kathy? She doesn't exist here."

"And you say I'm the high one. Why are you smoking that? It smells like death."

"I don't smoke like I did when I was young, I only do it now and then."

Her fingers quickly got lost in her frizz. "Do you think we could find a liquor store open somewhere around here?"

"I don't know."

"And then maybe we could get tattoos. Just one. We could match."

Poe spun sideways on his heels so he faced her. "No, Lily. You need to calm down. We're not getting drunk, and we sure as fuck aren't getting tattoos."

***

Lily sat slumped in a cushioned chair with her arm slung over the side. She clenched the neck of a small, cheap bottle of champagne. Her swan sat planted in her lap.

"What about a swan?" she said. "It seems appropriate."

"Fuck, no," Poe shouted, even though he was a mere few feet away from her in the second chair.

"Why not?"

"It's cliché. It's too much," he said as he cradled a glass bottle of *Grey Goose*. His speech was just as garbled as her's.

The tattoo artist had the image of a black and white skunk draped across the inside of his lower right arm. "Come on, guys. Just pick something. I wasn't even open today, I just had to get something before I went home."

"We'll pay you extra, obviously," Poe said as he poured another gulp of vodka into his mouth.

The skunk-tattooed man took a step back, clearly not sober himself. "Yeah, sure. Okay, thanks, man."

"I'm a dancer," Lily said.

"That's nice," the skunk-tattooed man responded.

"Maybe I could get pointe shoes on my foot or something."

"Cliché again."

"Why don't you look through the book again?" the skunk-tattooed man said.

He slid a leather-bound bundle of pages into her free hand. She sighed as she focused her blurred vision on the various illustrations and images. She flipped through the laminated pictures.

"I liked that one of a crescent moon that I saw," Poe rolled up his sleeve to reveal the image of a whale swimming down his arm. "Can you put it on my wrist?"

"Okay, sure," the man said and sidestepped over to Poe's chair.

Lily ran her index finger and thumb over the bottle's neck, resting the ebony book on the swan's plush body. "This tree is kind of cool."

"Can I see?" Poe asked.

She hoisted the book up and flashed the illustration to him. "The little bird in the leaves is cute."

He stared at it for a moment and blinked lazily. "It's alright. Get one that means something to you, I reckon that's the best advice I can give you with this kind of thing."

She continued thumbing through the pages until she found one that sucked the breath from her. She blinked and bent her head down to try and unearth a clearer image. She saw a stag's antlers with a bouquet of colored lilies, dandelions, roses, and peacock feathers.

"Found anything you like?" the man asked.

"Yeah, yes. I have, I like this one. I love this one."

He bent his head over his shoulder. "Oh, yeah, that's pretty. Where do you want it?"

She straightened her back. "Could I get it on my wrist, too?"

"Yeah, sure. Which one of you should I do first? The wrist hurts, to be honest."

Poe cleared his throat. "Do you want to go first?"

She fluttered her eyes between the skunk-tattooed man and Poe. "Yeah, I'll go."

"Great." He prepared his needle. "But this'll take some time, and you really should come back for a follow up."

Time weaned on and stretched. Minutes passed, and the needle made contact with the soft flesh on her arm. A flashing shot of lightning galloped up and through her veins. The brightness of the light burned at the back of her eyes. All at once, she transcended, and was taken away.

Chapter 10
The Future, Melody

I stroked my hand over the faded image of the stag's flowered antlers on my wrinkled wrist. Melody's heavy shoes plodded against my apartment floor.

"How are you feeling this morning, Lily?" Melody's voice was high-pitched, as though she was speaking to a child.

I craned my neck to look out of the window. A shooting pain trickled down the back of my head.

"I'm alright." I could hardly believe how ugly and weak my voice sounded. I hated the way it shivered.

"Do you think you'd like something to snack on before your guests come?"

"No, I think I'll wait. Thank you, dear."

It was strange, calling her 'dear.' The civility between us was still slightly awkward. I wondered if she even liked it when I called her 'dear.' I had no idea how to ask her.

"And they'll be here at 1:00?" she asked, clearly making conversation only to keep the silence at bay.

"1:00. And please, don't fuss. They won't need anything much."

"Of course," she said. "Would you like to go to the living room? I can put on a movie for you if you want, while I clean."

"That'd be nice. Thank you, dear."

I felt the dog's breath as he laid in an imprint in the space next to me. He had no idea that I would be gone in a few months. He would never even know what happened to me. I would just vanish, in a moment, as if I was never there. I wondered if he would even remember me. My heartbeat quickened and my stomach churned.

Melody grabbed the handles of my wheelchair. "Are you sure I can't bring you a platter of goat cheese, or even some crackers?"

"I'm not hungry just now."

"You didn't eat anything at breakfast. I know how sick that medication makes you on an empty stomach."

"If I need anything, I promise I'll tell you, dear."

She grew silent behind me and I knew she understood.

"Alright, then. I'll bring you some of that tea you like. You don't have to drink it if you don't want to."

I knew she remembered how it was when she first arrived, when I still had power over my legs. I knew she remembered the tantrums, the screaming, the things I called her during my fits, the medication I flushed down the toilet. I doubted she would ever forget it, no matter how many times I called her 'dear.'

"Thank you, Melody."

Maggie had been the one to hire her. She hadn't asked me. She had traveled all the way down to Florida without my knowing and had only made a few trips to a couple of different agencies before she had found Melody. And she left without seeing me. From what I gathered from Christmas cards, my sister had been holding up well, despite her age. She had nine grandchildren and a husband who died after being married to her for decades. I had not been invited to their wedding.

"I wish I liked tea." Melody parked my chair in front of the television. "Gabriel always wants me to drink it, he swears it fixes everything."

"Don't let your husband tell you what to do. It's a surefire way to get a divorce," I said.

Her eyes flashed up, then dropped back down. I surprised her, perhaps even offended her.

"We get along pretty well," she replied. "You know how it is. Everyone gets tired of each other sometimes."

"Yes?"

"Yeah, of course. It happens."

"Everything alright, dear?"

"I am — we are. Let me go make you that tea." She rushed off into the kitchen before I had the chance to say anything else.

I twisted my head to scan, then my gaze fell back to the television. Puck sat perched on the couch cushion, his tail swaying as he watched me. I know he must recall when I used to take him down to the beach on mild afternoons; when I let him loose to splash in the ocean. I wondered if it confused him, how vastly changed I was from a year ago. My fingers jerked and fluttered.

I wondered what Seraphina would do if she was alive. I wonder if she would recognize me now - an old woman. I never really thought I would get this old.

"Once you're done, dear, could you put my dog on my lap? I'd like to hold him."

"Of course, just a minute."

I watched as sunlight streamed in through the curtains, the wind blew against them gently. I wondered if I would remember sunlight, or wind, or the way they had once felt against my skin.

Melody stepped into the room. She placed my tea on a fold-out tray attached to my chair. Then she went toward the dog, reached down strangely and plucked him up. Her lips curled up in a sneer as her fingers clutched the animal. She plopped him in my lap and then scrubbed her hand on her jeans.

"Thanks so much, dear."

"Let me know if you want sugar in your tea."

"No, thank you. And you should rest. Sit down for just a moment. How has it been so far? Any morning sickness? Pains?"

She tucked some loose hairs back behind her ear. "I get pretty queasy when I first wake up, but it's not that bad."

All at once, I felt like a disguised, elderly mage. I wondered if she knew how little sense she made to me.

"How's Gabriel doing with it all?"

"He wants a little boy, of course. But I want a girl."

"But he's excited?"

She leaned deeply onto one foot and fidgeted with the hem of her jeans. "He's anxious. But I think he'll feel better once the baby's born."

"Dear —"

"You watch your movie, Lily. Relax. Don't worry about me."

My fingers shivered as they stoked over Puck's snowy fur. He used to hate being held. He used to twist and try to burst away from me. The years have relaxed him.

"I hate to ask you to do all this extra cooking, dear. Especially in your condition."

"Don't worry about it. Gabe expects a full course meal every night, so this isn't very much different." She laughed.

"I'd still like to give you a little something extra tonight."

I reached over to the handle of my chair and feebly clutched it. There was hardly an ounce of strength in my fingertips.

"God," I grunted.

"Lily? Everything alright?"

"Yes, I'm fine. Fine."

"Do you need anything?"

"I'm fine," I gasped. "Oh, God."

Her footsteps clicked through the tiled kitchen, then silence, and I know she had reached the gray carpet on the living room floor. A cool glass pressed itself into my hand. I pried my eyes open and saw Melody cradle a large, white tablet in her fingers.

"Take this, take it."

"My head…"

"Shh, shh. You know you'll feel better once you swallow it."

I could barely form a grip around the pill as I flung it into my mouth and felt it plummet down my throat with a splash of water.

"I told you, I'm fine," I said.

Melody had devolved into a shapeless blob, but I could see her back away. "Wait just a little while. It'll kick in soon."

"I know. I know."

"It's alright, it's okay."

"Can you lay me down, please? Let me take a little nap before they arrive."

My body folded over as I felt the pressure of her hand on my back and waist. I was rolled out onto my back on the couch, and I sunk onto the plushness of the sofa.

"Wake me up at 12:30. I want to put my wig on before they get here."

"Yes, of course. Try to relax."

My consciousness drifted in and out like a puff of smoke that flowed through one ear and out of the other. I knew that my sleep had not been steady because my eyes were dry and sagging when they pried open again. The sun had moved to a new position and the clouds had rolled in. Light was no longer flushed through the curtains. Melody had latched the windows closed. I did not feel the wind.

"Melody?"

"Yes? Are you ready to get up?"

"What time is it?"

"12:15. I'm glad you were able to have a little rest before they get here."

My back had cramped up, and my stomach and chest ached. I tried to push my legs over the side of the couch, but my muscles would not allow it.

"I'd like to put my wig on, dear."

"Lily, Lily, Lily, please wait. You don't want to hurt yourself right before they arrive."

She ran in and hoisted me back up into my chair. Puck was asleep on the couch cushion.

"Have you fed Puck? And not that canned shit."

She smiled. "Of course, don't worry about that. Do you want to change into something else?"

"Yes. The black pants and pink shirt. And the wig."

"Right. Let's go ahead and do that so we have plenty of time."

She pushed me into my room. The walls were painted a faded dusty-rose, the carpet was the lightest shade of pearl imaginable. I first moved in when I was thirty-nine, after I had returned from the Himalayas. That was after Seraphina had long forgotten about me. When my life with Seraphina ended, I had almost nothing as far as money. Seraphina handled the break better than me, she had been wanting it for some time. We fell out of touch fast, almost instantly. She was able to go on with her work in the mountains.

I had been staying in an old cabin of ours when I had snapped. I had traveled as fast as I could to the airport. I'm not sure why I had decided on the Himalayas. Perhaps I had hoped to find Seraphina's mother somewhere in those forests. And I had always liked the way 'Himalayas' felt against my tongue, velvet and silk coating the inside of my cheeks and jaw. It had been a one-way flight. Maybe I had been planning on killing myself once I got there. I had only known that I was free, and I could not cope with what that freedom had cost me.

"Is that comfortable?" Melody straightened out my blouse and swiped the creases away.

"Yes, thank you, dear."

She does not make much eye contact. But I never did either when I was her age. I did not know how old she was exactly. I had never asked. "Melody, dear?"

"Yes?"

"When is your birthday? I'd like to get you something special as a 'thank-you.'"

She laughed softly, and I saw how easily her husband could have fallen in love with her. "It's April 22nd, but you don't need to worry about getting me anything. I still can't quite believe I'll be twenty-seven this spring."

The very marrow in my bones seemed to crack as I tried to shift myself into a more comfortable position. "Please don't pretend that twenty-seven is old. That makes me ancient."

"You're not, don't talk like that."

I could not bring myself to smile, even in cordiality. "I know you've told me, but how long have you been married to your husband?"

"Oh, three years or so. Why do you ask?"

I glanced down to the wrinkled tattoo on my wrist, reaching my fingertips over to slosh the watery skin around. "No reason."

In the end, I had spent two years in the Himalayan Mountains. In the beginning, I had bathed and eaten whenever I could. At one time there had been enough money to do so almost at my leisure. I had been with Seraphina for nine years. It was shocking just how fast I spent what those nine years had given me. Almost a decade in capital evaporated into what felt like nothing after only a few months. I was thirty-seven. Most of what I had left was spent on a backpack and the supplies that filled it. Within the first sixty days, I had nearly died twice. I had not known what to do, I had not known why I had been doing it. It was not until I met the locals that I had decided to stay alive. I had to force myself not to break into their culture. So, I had observed from a distance. Existing in the mountains had been difficult. I was still not sure how I had survived at all. I could still remember the first time I had seen stars without light pollution. Perhaps that had been how.

"You know, I used to have hair this color," I said as Melody adjusted the blonde wig over my scalp, straightening it. I looked so much younger in that wig. It was strange to miss my hair. I also missed the way other women's hair felt against my fingers. I had loved men, a few here and there, but nothing compared to the way women smelled, the way their skin felt, the way their lips felt against mine. None of them had ever truly compared to Seraphina. She had died a long while ago, twenty years or so now - after years working and living on Lorelai. One of her horses had bucked her off, and she had shattered her head against a boulder. She included me in her will, leaving me little trinkets from the life I never shared with her. From what they told me, her death had been instant. I knew that would have pleased her.

I watched Melody as she grinned down at me from the mirror. "I've seen the pictures of you when you had hair this long. You were beautiful. You still are, of course."

"Nobody sees beauty in age."

Melody paused, her fingers hesitated over my skull. "Well, I think you've aged wonderfully. Really, I do."

By the end of my first year in the Himalayas, I had chopped off my hair into the pixie cut I had always wanted. I had convinced myself it was for the sake of convenience. It had looked hideous, choppy and uneven. Human interaction had swiftly become foreign to me. I liked to think that it was then that I made my peace with Jesus. We had said our goodbyes on a trailhead. It was romantic to imagine that I could pinpoint that down to a time, or a moment. But time folded in on itself when I was there. My flesh and the edges that defined my existence had become blurred. I was still not sure why I decided to return to the States after the end of the second year. Something had finished, I was never sure what. I became a creature fixed in space again. I woke up. A journey had ended, so I left. I never talked about the Himalayas, even when people asked.

"There's an old-fashioned clip I'd like to wear, a gold shell. Do you have any idea where it might be?" I asked.

It seemed silly to pin back a wig, especially when everyone knew that it was a wig.

"The one with black feathers?" Melody asked.

I nodded, my mouth drying. "That's the one."

"There are a couple of places it might be. Let me look around."

I chose to go to Florida because I had finished with the mountains. I was not angry anymore, or resentful. I was simply done. At first, I did not think I could handle being back in American civilization. The noise, the sounds, the smells all overwhelmed me. But I had the ocean. Maggie had, in my time away, sent me a bundle of money for birthdays and Christmases which had all been waiting for me when I returned. It was as though she had not noticed that I had been gone at all. The first thing I had purchased was a red bathing suit. It was too big. My hair had grown down to my shoulders, it had gotten wavier than before. I was thirty-nine by then, but my body was in good shape from the hiking. A few weeks had passed in a haze of mojitos and barefoot walks in the sand. I had calmed from my days in the Himalayas. I had finally been able to accept the price of my freedom. I had realized that it kept my soul from atrophying into rot.

"Here, Lily, is this the one you mean?" Melody held out the golden hair fork.

I could not even recall who gave it to me. "Yes. Perfect. Thank you, dear."

"Would you like me to put it in for you?"

"Would you? I always used to wear it on the left side."

It had been difficult for employers to stomach a gap in a resume as wide as mine. I had refused to put Seraphina down as a reference, so I had forced them to take my word for my time at the sanctuary on Lorelai. It took forty-two interviews before I secured a position. His was Liam, he was a seventy-nine-year-old florist with a dinky little flower shop on a street across from the ocean. He ran the place with his wife before ovarian cancer had claimed her. At the time, he did not tell me that he was dying, too. He liked that I was a little older and found it amusing that my name was Lily. It turned out that I had a talent for flowers. He allowed me to rent out the apartment above the flower shop. Some of the bouquets were wilted, and the air conditioning had been a joke. The perfumed scent had made me slightly queasy each time I walked through the glass doors. We usually ate lunch together in the break room, and sometimes he told me stories of his wife. We worked well together. We looked forward to seeing each other every day. We had never been outwardly affectionate, but we had an understanding. There was a bond between us. When he died, I had known him for a little over four years. He hadn't told me that he had been planning on leaving the shop to me. Still, I took it over. I kept the windows open for quite some time. I began adopting animals from the shelters. I became involved with a church whose choir was completely composed of drag queens. I became an eccentric spinster who people discussed fondly. And that was me for many decades.

I looked at myself in the mirror. I had chosen this wig because I had always wanted spiral curls. If I had to see myself with that bone-straight style again I doubt whatever was left of my sanity would have remained. Still, I selected blonde. I could have chosen black, red, pink. But I decided on blonde.

"Melody, would you take me back into the living room? I expect they'll be here any minute now."

"Yes, Lily."

I could hear the tiny 'm' forever strapped to the front of my name, always about to call me 'ma'am' but she resisted that urge. It was strange for her not to call me that. At the beginning, when she first came, it may have been her calling me 'ma'am' that rammed me over the cliff. She was not new to working with people like me, ushering elders into death. I could tell that she had wanted a limited familiarity with me, given that she would only know me for a few months at best. I had once despised her for it, an old flame had sparked in my stomach. I had not known anger like that in decades; a final burst of flames that nearly incinerated me entirely. Instead, I was left to flicker out, leaving nothing more than a puff of smoke to blow away in the wind.

"You didn't drink your tea. I think it does make you feel better when you drink it."

I looked over to the end table beside the couch as Melody parked me in front of the television.

"I told you that I didn't want it, dear."

"Yes, I know."

A hard rap suddenly slammed against the door, a shiver ran over my spine and my eyes watered. I clutched the handles of my chair.

"That's them."

"I'll get the door."

"Thank you, thank you," I replied, my voice crumbled.

Shepard entered first. It had only been a short while since I had seen him last, yet he appeared to have decomposed in that time. A corpse walking. Boyish good looks like his did not seem to age well. He had turned into one of those elderly men that wore too-tight pants and a polo shirt opened at the top so his gray chest hair stuck out. I remembered when his hair was thick and smooth, now it was sparse and gelled down in a comb-over. He shuffled when he walked, and for the first time, I realized that his life was nearly over, too. That made me sadder than I had expected it would.

"Hello, Lily," his voice tight and strained. "How are you feeling?"

"I'm fine, thank you, darling. Come here, let me see you."

He wrapped fingers delicately around mine. He was scared of me, I knew. He understood the situation, he understood that this was the only future left to him. I could not bear his fear, I wished I could have removed it from him; flushed it out.

"How are you?"

"I'm dying, my love, how do you expect me to be?"

His face fell, but I smiled wider.

"Is there much pain?"

I rubbed the back of his knuckles with my cracked fingertips. "It's alright. I promise it's alright."

I heard a click that emanated from the doorway, and that's when he stepped in. His once ebony hair had been swept into a white mane, curled and dangling down to his earlobes. The snowy shade brought out the blue in his eyes. Beautiful, lovely. Always. His skin had a few more wrinkles than would be expected for a man his age, but he had kept his body in check as best he could. He was still stunning; he would always be stunning. He smiled at me and I fell in love with his crooked teeth all over again.

"Hello," he said, rushing to kiss me on the forehead.

He tilted his skull down slightly, so the front of our heads rested against each other. He closed his eyes, but I kept mine open. I wanted to see all of him. I had not noticed that my hands had broken away from Shepard's until they were intertwined with Poe's. His palms were soft, velvet. They filled me with calm, bliss. I could not recall the last time he had been that affectionate with me.

"Hello, you crazy man."

"Doesn't she look wonderful, Shep?" he said.

He nodded feebly. His cloudy eyes scanned me over.

"I have lunch ready for you all. Would you like to eat in the kitchen?" Melody called.

"Yes, I think that'll be fine, dear," I said.

Melody stepped forward to grab my chair. Poe launched toward me before she could reach the handles.

"Can I push her?"

Melody hesitated for a moment. "Yeah, sure."

I scoffed and waved him off with my fingers, pretending not to be touched by his gesture. He quickly rolled me over to my little wooden table, the one I had purchased at a flea market for $25. The speed made me queasy. I imagined that my carved dining table would end up in another flea market, and one day it would be purchased again, where it would sit in another apartment. Perhaps a family of three would haul it home in the back of their truck.

Melody laid out the plates and food and filled up our glasses with water. I thanked God that I could still eat and drink on my own. I would never have invited any of them if I could not at least do that. Shepard sat parallel to my wheelchair. Poe perched himself directly beside me.

No matter where I had traveled after Meadowlark, no matter who I was or what I did, Poe had always been there. Poe never left. I could have been half of a world away, we might not have communicated for six months, but I would always find him again. And he would always find me. I had loved him, just as I had loved Shepherd for loving him.

My hand ached from gripping the water glass.

The three of us did not speak. We had talked all of our lives. There was nothing left to say. We were tired, all of us. Still, I enjoyed feeling them near me. I knew that I would never see them again. Yet, I could not fathom an existence without them. I was leaving them, and it terrified me.

"Do you need anything, Lily?" Melody stepped behind my chair.

I straightened my back, and it felt as though dirt was being piled over my head. Suddenly, I hated them for staying all weekend. I hated my skin, I hated my wheelchair, and I hated the way my voice sounded.

I hated that I could still feel my feet and my legs. I hated the aches and sores. I hated that I could still remember what my feet could do when the Firebird possessed them. I hated that I still hated. I hated that the fire had not burnt out by then.

"Yes, could you take me outside for just a moment?"

I saw the three of them glance up to me in confusion. I was so terrified that I would break in front of them. I did not want whatever was left of the flame to seep out from the cracks and burn them. I had worked too hard to keep the blaze under control to allow it to consume me. I would not die as a charred piece of meat.

"Yeah, of course, Lily," Melody said.

I was wheeled by them, a flash of blue from Poe's eyes rushed passed my gaze. The hall led out to the balcony and buried me. I wanted to run, but I could not. I wanted to breathe, but I would not soon. Melody pushed me out into the air, and the wind embraced me. I closed my eyes.

"Thank you, thank you, dear," I said.

"Sure, no worries," she told me. I could hear her discomfort. "Are you feeling alright?"

"Are you happy with your husband?" I opened my eyes to look at her.

"Yes. Of course. We're married, we're happy."

"You don't seem happy."

She folded her arms over her stomach. "I think I will be, soon. I was happy with him, at one point. I don't see why I can't be again."

I could feel air circulating through my lungs again. "You know the swan in my room? The stuffed animal?"

She cocked one brow. "I do, yes."

"Would you mind taking it with you? When you go home tonight?"

"I couldn't do that, I -"

"Please, for your child." Did she understand how little time we had left?

Her grin faded. "Can I ask you something?"

"Yes."

"Have you been happy?"

"With what? With you?"

Melody shifted from one foot to the other. "Have you been happy?"

She did not attempt to make eye contact. "I'm sorry if I've offended you."

I stared for a moment, and then turned away.

"I think we need to get Puck out for a little while this afternoon," she said.

"That's a good idea."

"Maybe the four of us can go down to the park by the shore."

"Did you know that Jack's little girl is getting Puck?"

She nodded.

"She can't wait for me to go so she can get him."

"Lily, you know that's not —"

"I hate her for taking him from me."

"Puck will have a good home. She loves him already."

My eyes blurred with tears. "It'll be so easy to forget about me."

"No, it won't. I'll give your swan to my baby. It won't forget you. Because of that."

"The swan isn't real. It's just a stuffed animal."

"Lily."

"I'm dying," I said. "The swan isn't real. I'm dying."

Melody was scared of me, that was why she never had really touched me, why she could not stand the sight of me. I was Death. I was infected and polluted. My body was decaying. I was rot. I was so terrified that I would not remember the taste of Jasmine rice, or Pierre and Natasha, or what it felt like to swim in the ocean at night. I was so terrified that the fire would outlive me. I was terrified that my plush swan would be all that was left of me.

"I'll make sure my baby knows you, I promise."

For a moment, perhaps for many moments, neither of us spoke. My fingers stretched out, reaching for her. I loved her, I wished I could repay her.

"Is that true?"

"Yes, ma'am."

My eyes filled with tears again. I did not let them fall. "Thank you, thank you, even if you're lying."

"I should go inside," she whispered. "I'll offer them some tea, it'll keep them occupied for a little while. You can just take a moment out here. I'll only take you back when you're ready." I heard her shuffling beside me. "I'll come back and check on you in a few minutes, okay?"

"Yes. Thank you, dear."

I listened as she sighed slowly through her nose. The heels of her shoes clicked against the balcony wood. "Try to enjoy the fresh air."

"Yes. Thank you, dear."

I did not know how to tell her that I had fallen in love with her. I could not understand her, not really, just as she could not understand me. Not anymore.

"Did you hear that NASA has lost communication with the Voyager crafts?" she asked.

"What?"

"It was on the news. NASA has severed communication with Voyager. They've gone too far into space. I thought you'd like to know."

I wanted to reach out and touch her hand, but my muscles would not allow it. I wished I could have kissed her.

"Yes. Thank you, dear."

"No worries."

Melody turned and left the balcony. I looked back out at the view and into the garden. The flowers were already dying without my care. I needed to stand up. The muscles in my legs were atrophied so deeply, I was not sure they would hold my weight for even a few seconds. My body had rebelled against me, or perhaps it was simply shutting down, like a machine exhausted from overuse.

I grabbed the rails and pushed my fingers into the damp, rotting wood. I groaned and dropped my head back as I hoisted myself upward. My arms simmered with muscle strain. I mashed my teeth together and threw the weight of my body up against the railing. My knees buckled, but I relied on the strength of my upper body to keep myself afloat. I looked down at my perishing garden and saw a lump.

It had been a long time since I had seen him, truly seen him. There had been bad days when I had caught momentarily glimpses of him, or when I felt his fur rub up against the lining of my stomach, but the medication and therapy and institutions had kept us apart for many years. For the first time, I felt pride as it blossomed in my chest. Did I have a right to be proud? I was not sure. I cocked my head as I watched him breathe raggedly and with great struggle. He did not look afraid, he looked peaceful. The wind blew through his fur, weaving through it as though it were shards of grass. I believed I loved him a little bit. I thought perhaps something in me understood him for the first time. I watched as he twisted his head back, and I caught a tiny glimpse of his eye.

Had I been happy?

I dropped back down into my chair. My head burned with the itch from the wig. I reached my hand underneath it. Melody would adjust it for me before I went back in. My stubby fingernails scratched against my scalp. It is there that I felt a bump.

I had always known I would become a stag.

"My battery is low," I said. "And it's getting dark."

***

"What do you think? Not bad, I'd say." The skunk-tattooed man said.

Lily blinked rapidly as the light drained from the back of her eyes. "What?"

"Don't go swimming for at least two weeks. It'll peel and get all scabby if you do."

Lily's head pounded as she looked down at the image of the stag's antlers on her wrist.

"What happened? It's already done?"

"I mean, yeah. You did really well with the pain."

She closed her eyes, grimaced and folded her hand over her heart, feeling as though it had ruptured in her chest.

"Lily? Hey, you alright?"

She flung the other arm that had not been illustrated up to the top of her skull, rooting her fingers through her dry hair. She tried to feel for the lump on the side of her skull, yet there was nothing.

"Yes. I'm fine."

"Do you like your tattoo?" Poe slurred.

She swallowed, blinked rapidly in an attempt to clear her eyes. "I…"

"Oh fuck," the skunk-tattooed man said. "You don't like it."

She looked up at him. "No, I love it."

"Oh. Oh?"

"I love it. I do."

She could hardly see it. Her vision was still fogged. She reached her thumb over to glide across the illustration. It was red and swollen and stung at the pressure of her touch. Still, it was lovely. The colors were vibrant, the details were drenched in clarity.

"Can you do mine now? Before I sober up." Poe flashed his wrist to the skunk-tattooed man.

He stepped over to fetch a new needle. "Yeah, sure."

When Lily's eyes were finally cloudless, she could hardly stop staring at the new colors that decorated her wrist. Her flesh had been altered forever.

"I think my liver is shutting down, like, right now." Poe flung his head back and allowed it to rest against the rim of the leather chair.

"Just don't haunt my shop," he said while he prepared Poe's skin.

Lily looked back up to the mirror and put her fingertips against her jawline. She had a nice chin. The bone was cut sharply. It kept her neck from appearing too short and emphasized her facial structure. She had never noticed that before. She lifted her hand further to skim across her nose. It was sprinkled with freckles and pointed upward near its narrow tip. She had her mother's nose. She had always hated her nose.

Her mother came from a strong Russian family who all had the pointed, upturned noses. Lily's grandmother barely spoke English, her grandmother's parents were dead before they had arrived in America. Lily could remember how her father glared at her grandmother before she died, and when they were at her funeral, she had heard her father whisper to a friend, "The casket cost $3,000. Can you fucking imagine?" And then he had made the sign of the cross over his forehead and chest.

Lily's grandmother lost too much and never quite recovered. She had blanketed herself in a thin layer of ice and allowed herself to freeze over. She could never allow the fire to reach her. She would rather die from the frost than burn alive. It was an easier death, Lily knew. Less painful, more peaceful.

Lily had never understood her grandmother. Her grandmother had never understood her. They had always been aliens to one another. They spoke two entirely different languages. There had been no communication between them, neither of them had been willing to learn the other's tongue. A grudge had boiled against her grandmother for cursing Lily with that nose. Yet, now, for the first time, she stared at their nose. She stared at the narrowness, at the uneven bends and curves. She had never considered herself a beauty, she had never even allowed herself to believe that she was pretty. But her grandmother had once complimented her eyes, and everyone always told her that her greatest feature was her hair. Now her hair was gone, she would never allow it to grow back. She should have been plain without her hair. She should have been ugly. Perhaps she was. Could she allow herself to enjoy her jawline and her nose? Did she have the right?

The cartilage in one's nose never ceases to grow in the whole human life. One day, her nose would become wrinkled and old. She closed her eyes and pressed her fingertips against her nose. The tip was chilled against her touch. She heard Poe and the skunk-tattooed man mutter in their places beside her. She could not focus on their words. She was unsure if it was the marijuana or the alcohol. Her senses were obscured, so much so that she felt she was at risk of dissolving into the leather chair, and her skin and bones would melt into the scuffed floor. She placed her shoes flat on the tile, folded her arms over her stomach, and allowed her eyes to fall over the ceiling. Stars were directly above her, but the roofing shrouded them from her.

Chapter 11
The Present, Aurora

"It hurts like fuck. If I get an infection, I'm suing."

"You're fine," Lily smiled a little.

"I don't want my wrist to fall off."

Every morsel of Lily's high was wearing away. The world around her was once again impenetrable. Her arms hung in weights at her side and her feet scuffed against the ground. The skin on her face felt heavy.

"You're being dramatic."

Poe had become frustrated at their impending sobriety. His back had curved. He wobbled as he walked, though not significantly.

"I wonder if Kathy has called the cops."

"I don't know, I doubt it. Can you imagine if the news heard about you? The tabloids would collectively lose their minds if they found out. Aren't you still famous?" Lily looked up at him.

"I'm only famous in the bad way."

"The Doctor wouldn't want Meadowlark to get any bad press, he'd rather let us perish out here," she said.

"He can't be that hateful," Poe replied.

She watched him as he walked. "I didn't say he was. I never said that."

Poe's eyes drifted down to her's. "Do you want to sit down? You look tired."

"Yes. And then I think we should go back. We could call a taxi."

"You want to go back to the prison?" Poe said, a hint of surprise in his voice.

"You said it wasn't a jail, that we could leave at any time or something like that."

His gaze drifted from her. "I know."

"We have to go back. I don't know why. We just do."

He hesitated before he shrugged. "Fine. I can't believe how little I care anymore."

Lily looked through the opacity of the night. Her mother would scream if she saw her wander sloppily through a public park. Every now and then they would stroll past a raggedy man or woman collapsed drunkenly on the crusted brown grass. Lily was surprised by how little snow had lasted through the morning, and how warm the winter night was. They rounded a corner, and an archway of electric Christmas lights came into view. Her eyes fixed on a wooden brown bench at the base of the arch. It had been newly painted.

"Let's sit here."

"Right." Poe flung himself against the seat.

"My feet are bleeding, I think," she said.

"I left mine back at the tattoo parlor."

Lily laughed. It echoed through the park. She covered her palm over her mouth to stifle the sound. "I'm going to get us arrested."

"There aren't any cops out tonight. Anyway, they'd never waste their time on bums like us."

"We're not bums."

"Vagrants?"

"We're both too rich to have the right to call ourselves that."

He chuckled through his nose. "I won't be rich after all this. Going crazy is only for those who can afford it."

"You should post that somewhere."

He grinned and then slid his fingers through his hair. "What about you? Aren't your parents farmers or something?"

"My father is. My mother works at an elementary school."

"Jesus. A wholesome American family."

She nibbled on the inside of her cheek. "It would have been without me."

"So, how do you afford it? Meadowlark."

"My great aunt died," she said. "She gave her money to my parents, they used it to get rid of me. Is that a fee or an investment?"

He pursed his lips. "They don't want to -"

"Yes, they do," she said, not making eye contact. "They did."

He pressed his spine against the back of the bench. "I guess Shepard did it to me, too. I don't reckon people like us are easy to take. Maybe we're impossible to take. People who don't understand us can't be around us for very long. We make them crazy. The only people who do understand are like us, and we're all too trapped in our heads to do much of anything for long. We're stuck."

Her head felt too heavy for her neck to support. She wondered if it could possibly roll off her shoulders and disappear into the snow. She glanced up at the lights strung over the top of the arch. "Do you ever think about Voyager 1?"

"No. I remember you said something about it in group once."

She crossed her arms over her chest. "I took an astronomy class in high school. That was the first time I heard of it. It was the first manmade object to leave the heliosphere. Have you heard of the Golden Record?"

"Heard of it, yeah."

"Do you know what it is?"

"No, not really. Wasn't it made by the *Cosmos* guy?"

"Carl Sagan."

"Him, yeah."

She nodded. "*The Sounds of Earth*, that's what they called it. They put a recording of the Navajo Native Americans singing *Night Chant*, Solomon Islands panpipes, Beethoven. They put a whale song in." Her voice broke away and she began to chuckle.

"What?" Poe said.

"I remember my teacher told us that Europa had an ocean underneath that layer of ice. Did your teachers ever tell you that? I always imagined that there was one whale under there that people on Earth couldn't see. I don't know why. It doesn't make sense. But I always thought that, when the Voyager passed over Europa, somehow the whale could hear it. I thought maybe it could hear the Golden Record and the whale song and know that we're here."

Poe shifted in his seat, like a child waiting for the next chapter of a story. "I don't think that's silly."

She curled her fingers into a fist. Her cheeks grew warm from the smoke in her bones. "I'm not making any sense. I'm too tired." She blinked lazily, her eyelids struggled to rise again once they had shut. "I'm so tired, aren't you tired?"

"Yes."

She slanted her head so her temple rested on his shoulder. "Do you ever wonder if you'll end up happy?"

He leaned his cheek against her pillowy hair. "I don't know if I'll ever really be happy. I like to think I'll be content. I just want peace."

"I'm not sure if it's worth it; all of this."

"Don't think like that. Thinking like that is what got me into Meadowlark in the first place."

Her eyes fell to the gravel pathway. "Not thinking about it'll kill you. It'll make you even crazier."

She felt him jolt as he laughed. "And what about you? Do you think you can be happy?"

"Sometimes I think I can see my future. Sometimes I think I know what'll happen. Even then, I can't tell if there's happiness. Every time I think I get close to an answer, it's like I wake up."

"The happiness wouldn't be real if you did. You know that."

She swallowed, and her eyes dropped out of focus. "I wish I knew where the Voyager will go after we lose contact."

"I don't think we deserve to know. It has to be enough that it's out there at all, that aliens might stumble across it someday."

She blinked sluggishly. "I'm never sure if I want anyone to find it. I think it should be like an epilogue."

Poe slid closer to her. He pressed his arm into hers. "You're too romantic, love."

"I'm so tired."

"I thought you wanted to get back to Meadowlark."

"I do. We should leave now," she said.

"No, just rest for a moment. Just rest. I doubt they'll even know we're gone."

The night wind brushed through her hair as the electronic lights twinkled above her, glowing just beyond her closed eyelids. It was chilly, not cold. And, in the fever of sleep, she could not be sure if it had happened at all.

***

"Do you understand what we went through last night?" Maggie shouted. Her hands were pressed into her hips. "Do you even care?"

Lily massaged her left temple with her index and middle fingers. "I thought The Doctor only called you, like, two hours ago."

"It was a long fucking two hours, you believe me."

She grimaced. "Can you please be a little quieter?"

"No," she screamed. "And what in the fuck did you do to your hair? You look like Tonya Harding."

The Doctor rolled his hands together. "I'm sorry, Margaret, but I'm not sure how helpful this is for her. We wouldn't want to send her over the edge."

"She knows how unforgivable this is. She knew what she was doing and she did it anyway."

"Margaret, please."

Lily glanced out the window nearest to them. "Maggie…"

"No. You don't get to speak."

"Margaret…" the Doctor continued.

"What was our mother supposed to think? And our father? They'd thought you'd been murdered or kidnapped or sold into the white sex trade."

"Did they think it was a Christmas miracle?" Lily asked.

"Lily," she cried. Even The Doctor's jaw fell slack.

Lily leaned back in her chair. "Sorry." She could hardly believe that she was devolving so soon.

"No, you're not. You never are." Maggie crossed her arms, then placed them on her hips again, and then allowed them to hang loosely at her sides. "I think you should come back home, but father and mother are finding this latest stunt pretty hard to forgive."

Lily's chest began to burn. "Are they?"

"Yes. They spend all that money from Great Aunt Katherine's estate on you, Lily, and this is how you repay them?"

"I never wanted to come here in the first place. Besides, I like Tonya Harding."

"She was a bitch who bashed in her friend's knee."

"She didn't do it herself. It was her husband."

"But she let it happen. Everyone knows that. Even if she didn't, she withheld information. That isn't suspect to you? She was trailer trash."

Lily tilted her chin up. She ran her left palm and fingers over her hair. "It was just getting too long."

Maggie blinked wildly. She flailed her arms upward. "What the fuck are we even talking about? What's wrong with you? Why are you like this?"

Lily fixed her gaze back toward the window. "I'm just tired."

Maggie faced The Doctor. "I can't believe this. We've given you a fortune to fix her, and she's worse than before."

"It's a process, Margaret."

"Well, I expect you to do something about this. What are our options at this point?"

"Maggie." Lily forced her voice to remain even and smooth. "I'm not going home."

Maggie snapped her head over to look at her, her brown ponytail flung back over her shoulders. "What? Are you saying you want to stay here?"

She swallowed the ball of saliva in her throat. "No. But I'm not going back to the farm. I never will. I mean that."

"You're being ridiculous, hysterical. Once you cool down…"

Lily shook her head. "No. I'm not saying that I'll never talk to mom and dad again, or to you. I'm just saying that I'll never live at the farm again. It's gone for me. I'm not being crazy or stupid. Something is over, finished. If you'd let yourself, you'd feel it, you'd know it too."

"I get it. You're blaming us for this. It's not our fault that you're crazy."

"Margaret, come now." The Doctor called, his voice wavered. "That kind of language is not conducive to mental healing."

"You understand that we've done everything we can for you? We've done all that we can. None of us can take this anymore." She put a heavy emphasis on each word.

Lily's being vibrated. Her cheeks flushed. Her body beaded over with sweat. She looked once more out of the window and saw him. He stood with his teeth bared; low to the ground. He looked hungry again. If he fed on her now, he would devour her sister, too. Lily mashed her teeth together as sweat began to drip down her back. A hint of something bright flashed over the Beast's eyes.

"I can't take it either. I can't take you, and mom, and dad, and that farm. There's no air there, everything is blurry and hazy, like I don't have enough oxygen in my brain," Lily said.

"So it *is*, our fault, then?"

"No, but I can't live like this anymore. I don't think you realize it, but being there is just making it worse. I don't know if I deserve to get better, but what's the point of my staying like this? Maybe I'll deserve it if I earn it."

"You get drunk once and now you're a fucking philosopher? You were never like this before."

"I thought that's what you wanted. I thought you wanted me different. Fixed."

"I want you better."

"You don't want me at all, Maggie."

"You're being so stupid."

Lily was still for a moment. She saw the Beast loom on the other side of the glass. "I need you to go for a while. I don't know how long. A while."

"Lily—" Maggie began.

She clicked her canine teeth together. "I want to be your friend one day. Really. I want us to be happy with each other. We just aren't there yet. We won't be there for a long time, I think. Both of us need time."

Maggie turned to The Doctor. "Get her on meds. I know I said I didn't want it, but I'm not sure what choice we have now."

"Oh, I see," he said. "Well, that is quite a big step. We have a great number to choose from. We'll start mixing up a cocktail for her."

"Get out, Maggie," Lily said gently. "I mean it, please, leave. I'm not angry, I don't blame you. I don't blame mom or dad. But there's something I've got to decide. You can't be a part of it."

She looked to Lily, then back at The Doctor. "Fine, I'm going. I'm going. I'll call tomorrow once you've cooled down."

"I won't answer. Tomorrow's too soon."

"Make sure gets medicated as soon as possible." Maggie tossed her ponytail over her shoulders.

"I really have always loved you, Maggie," Lily said. She was unsure if Maggie had not heard her or had simply pretended not to, but she fled the room without offering a reply.

The Doctor's mouth had risen into a tentative grin as he glanced back to Lily. "Well, I think you handled that very well. Very mature. No tantrums. You're making wonderful progress, as I've been saying. Why not go back to the common room and watch *The Wizard of Oz*? I know how much you love that movie."

Her gaze flickered away from the Doctor and back toward the window. He had evaporated from her sight. She knew the Beast was still there, hiding. She ripped a small piece of the flesh from her lower lip.

"He's watching me," she said.

The soundwaves from her words lingered in the thin air above them. She wondered if The Doctor had even heard her.

"Seraphina should be here for your ride soon," he said, his voice gentle and high-pitched, as though he spoke to a child.

Lily blinked. "When is she coming?"

"She should be here in about an hour."

"I'm tired. Can I go now? Can I go back to my room?"

"Yes, of course."

She despised herself for asking his permission.

She headed toward her room quickly, not stopping in the common room to check for Poe. She traveled through the hallways, and once she reached her room she climbed onto her bed. She smoothed down her hair as she allowed her head to fall onto the pillow. Her hair was reverting back to bone-straight and was losing some of its fluffy curls.

She lifted her wrist and examined the reddened tattoo. It was irritated, but not bloated with pain. It was lovely, and she smiled at the sight of it. She could hardly wait to show it to Seraphina. She would adore it.

The silence of the room suddenly settled down upon her. She focused only on the breath rising and falling in her chest. She did not intend on falling asleep, she only thought to rest her eyes. Yet, within moments, an edge of her subconscious pieced softly through her brain. Visions danced underneath her eyelids. A girl, lovely, with a wide smile and coiled curls. She crossed her legs at the ankles when she laid down. Natasha and Pierre. In the bed next to her's.

Lily's eyes snapped open. Vines of dread grew and spread all throughout her body and limbs. She had not always been alone. There used to be someone else in the room, she could almost remember her. She sat up.

"Aurora," she said.

Where was she? When was the last time she had seen her? No matter how long the days had felt, Lily knew she had been at Meadowlark for a little less than a month. Yet, every trace of Aurora was gone. Detailed memories washed over her, flooded every cell of her brain. Her messy bed, her copy of *War and Peace*, her pink pajamas. There was nothing left. Lily sprinted toward the doorway. Surely The Doctor or Nurse Kathy knew. Why had no one told her? Why had an announcement not been made? Her hands landed on the door frame. A chord inside her chest held her back. She turned and looked at the space Aurora had once occupied.

Aurora was gone before Lily ever knew her. Lily wrapped her fingers around her throat. She began to hum, tiptoeing slowly back into the room. Her own voice was eerie, spectral even. She knew that Aurora was not there. She had not been there for a long time. She looked back out the window. The woods. She threw her palm up over her mouth.

"Oh, God."

She pushed the door shut and went to her closet. She threw on her sweater. The fabric rubbed against her skin softly for the first time in many days. She cherished the comfort of it. It was warm, solid. Lily pressed her hands against the window. Although her room was on the first floor, it was still locked. She trembled furiously as she glanced around, careful not to be caught. An image rushed before her. There was a small pole inside of the closet, tucked beneath a loose piece of wallpaper.

Once the window had been shattered at the top right corner, there was a bolt that could be lifted, and the window would pry open. She moved slowly into the closet, dropped down to her knees, and skimmed her fingers below the wall. The tips of her flesh stung with the rough cold of rusted metal. She bent down and pulled the rod out. She looked back toward the window, rising from her knees. She angled one end of the pole toward the glass. She held her breath before driving the rod into the window. It only fractured at first. She looked back at the door, stopping momentarily to wait and see if anyone had heard her. Her gaze swiftly returned to the window, and she slammed the pole into it again. The glass burst apart in the upper right corner, creating trails of cracks that splintered off.

She reached her hand through the hole. Her skin nicked the edges, but her fresh tattoo had not been sliced severely. Tiny droplets of blood flowered onto the sweater sleeve, crimson mingled with plum. She unlatched the bolt and the window clicked. She looked to the left side of the frame. There was not a lock on that side. After Aurora had done this, they had not replaced it properly.

She pulled her arm through the glass, lifting the window before stepping through. The sun dipped down below the horizon, but it was not quite dark enough for the stars to shine yet. The wind was chilled and sharp. Her shoes crunched down into the old snow. The ice was firm and stiff, but her weight still broke through. It had begun to melt earlier that day, but the air had frozen over from the falling sun, and the snow had frosted with it. Tomorrow it would begin to thaw again.

She did not turn to look back at Meadowlark. It felt strange, a jailbreak. Terror penetrated her, and the vastness of the world and the woods made her head spin. She looked up at the clouded sky. She wished she could see the stars.

She wrapped her arms around her stomach. She did not want to walk forward, but she knew that Aurora was waiting for her. She was too frightened of forgetting again to go back into their bedroom. She ducked her head. The wind wrapped its bitter-cold gentle arms over her shoulders and lovingly pushed her toward the forest. It waited just ahead. She shivered and hummed a song that had been in her head for as long as she had been alive. She had never thought to sing it until that moment. Her shoes pressed against the ice, the ends of her toes froze as she did. She went deeper into the woods, an implacable fear made her nauseous.

She had been there before.

The tree branches above her laced their fingers together in a veil that blotted out the sky. If the stars were to come out, she would never know. She inhaled sharply through her nose. She kept humming. The blackness of the night continued to consume her as she traveled through the forest toward nowhere, only going to where she knew Aurora was.

"Hovan, Hovan Gorry og O

Gorry og, O, Gorry og O

Hovan, Hovan Gorry og O

I've lost my darling baby, O…" she sang.

"I found the swan upon the lake

Upon the lake, upon the lake

I found the swan upon the lake

But never found my baby, O…"

"Hovan, Hovan Gorry og O

Gorry og, O, Gorry og O

Hovan, Hovan Gorry og O

I never found my baby, O…"

She paused, her teeth chattered noisily.

"Aurora," she whispered hoarsely.

She turned to the right. That is what Aurora had done. The forest was just vast enough that someone could get lost and never be found; that was what Aurora had wanted.

Aurora Marnie had disappeared in January. No one had seen her from the morning of the 12th until the evening of the 18th. They got a great deal of criticism for that, for not keeping better track of their patients. The criticism was quickly forgotten.

Aurora had destroyed the window with a pole she had found outside. They were doing renovations at the time, and a builder had dropped it without realizing what he had lost. Aurora had plucked it from the ground and shoved it down her pants leg. She had been lucky that day. Security had only patted her down from the torso up. She had hidden the pole in her closet, tucking it underneath a rolled-up section of wallpaper. She had been unsure why she had not just chucked it in the woods after she had broken the window. Perhaps she had been afraid of getting lost completely. Perhaps she had wanted someone to know. To find out; to find her.

Lily doubled over as her stomach churned and bubbled. Without significant warning, vomit pierced through her lips and onto the snow. She whipped her back upright again and turned away from the mess in disgust. Aurora had been queasy, nauseous, and she had done that, too. Lily's quivering hand rose to press against her lips. She looked up at the sky again. The sun would never rise, not for her. Not for either of them. Her song would always be trapped in that forest with Aurora, circling, trying to find a hint of the sky. The stars would always be hidden, even those that were merely the twilight of dead suns.

Lily's feet trampled through the crusted snow and her spirit fell back behind her body. She knew that the world still turned. She felt the weight of gravity as it kept her feet pressed to the ground. Yet, she was no longer a part of it, she did not exist along with everything else. The quiet grass under her feet, the stags and fawns who searched for warmth and waited for spring, the bears who slept the winter away, she could not comprehend them. She watched herself as she wandered toward Aurora. She hummed and sung gently to no one. She closer, closer than the police ever had. She passed a large sycamore. Its trunk bent slightly to the side. She placed her hand against the bark. She moved around it before she saw the tree. Aurora had picked it because of the notch at the base of the trunk. It was the perfect place to step up and secure the rope around a branch. The notch would not have been strong enough to catch her when she dropped down. The last thing Aurora had felt was the edge of the trunk as it scrapped against her calf.

A hand gently brushed up against Lily's shoulder. She turned. Aurora's bright eyes looked passed her.

"My bones are down there, by the root," she signed.

Tears gathered behind Lily's eyelids. "How long? How long have you been there?"

Aurora glanced back up to the tree. "The rope rotted off a while ago. It was buried underneath the leaves and ice."

"Why did you do it? Why did you leave the pole in the closet?"

"My doctor hadn't even realized that I was gone, for days. By then, I was already decomposing."

Lily's knees buckled as she collapsed. Her palms slammed through the ice. She scrambled over to the root of the tree. She began to dig. It did not take long for her fingertips to go numb.

Aurora gazed back at her. "You can never find all of me. The Earth ate me and forgot about me."

Dirt and grime buried themselves underneath Lily's nails as droplets of her blood trickled onto the snow. She pressed her elbows down, forcing pressure to dig deeper and faster until her fingers fell against something hard. It was yellowed white and stood out against the snow. She plucked it up and smoothed her thumb over it, her eyes darted over its sharpened tip frantically.

"Part of my rib," Aurora said.

Lily's hand jolted to the side as the bone tumbled out of it and back onto the ground.

"It's too late," Aurora said.

Lily's breathing stalled for a moment, and she felt the silence as it washed over her. She collapsed back on her tailbone. She looked down at the spot where her corpse was buried. Flesh, sharp breath flew in her chest again, its wings batted against the walls of her lungs.

"How? When? How long? I don't understand."

Aurora dropped down onto her knees. "Meadowlark used to be called Ivy-House. Before the laws changed, it was a place to send people away for cheap. Everyone could forget about you and it barely cost anything."

"Who sent you?"

"My mother."

Lily's heart slowed. It moved at such a pace she worried it would halt altogether. "Why?"

"She could handle my being deaf. She could handle that I was mute. But she could never understand why I was crazy. Not being able to hear or talk was something she could blame on fate. But my brain was sick, and she was always confused why I could never heal myself. She was always tired because of me."

"You did it because of her?"

"No."

"Then why?"

"My brother. My brother, he never questioned why I was the way I

156

always was. He wanted me to be better, but I never could be, and he learned how to accept that. He was brave, the rest of the world was angry that he was brave. I adored him. No matter what, I thought I would have him. The day he died, we were walking down a sidewalk next to a candy shop. We stopped, just for a minute, so he could smoke a cigarette. The lady who owned the candy shop thought we were lingering, so she called the police. The policeman said we had to leave. He thought I was giving him an attitude because I never answered him when he spoke. Then my brother and him were arguing about something, and then we were running. He was beside me. Right beside me. And then he jolted forward. When I looked over, he had fallen behind. I realized that the policeman had shot him. I think I watched him die, but I don't remember. I barely remember anything. The only thing I can really see when I think about him is the way his eyes looked when he realized that he was going to be dead soon. The lady who owned the candy shop accused him of stealing, so nobody cared that he was dead. He was erased and I became invisible. My brother was my mother's hope. When I lost him, I lost her. For good. I know that she didn't have any choice besides sending me away, I thought I was making her crazy like me."

Lily dug her thumbnail into her palm. It tingled with pain, but the skin did not break. "Could you not have just run away? Start over? Leave your mother behind?"

"It wasn't her fault. You know that. I told you."

"You blamed yourself. Is that why you did it?"

Aurora's eyes drifted to her burial spot. "I hardly remember my brother. I hardly remember what it felt like to be alive. All I know is that I wanted to stop feeling, and I got what I wanted. I have no memory of pain, or joy, or love. I have no memory of excitement, of dread. Of guilt. All I feel now is emptiness, vastness in my stomach that consumes me like a void. People come into Meadowlark, some of them see me. I get stuck, I forget. Then they forget about me, because it always happens that way."

"I could never forget about you."

Beams of light shone in Aurora's eyes again. "You did. You did forget."

Lily's breath hitched as it drew in tightly through her lips. "But I remembered. I remembered you."

Aurora's face hardened. "You are not my savior," she signed, her fingers tight.

"I know. I never said that I was."

"Yes, you did. Just remember me," Aurora said. "All I need is for you to remember."

Lily pursed her lips, blinking rapidly to clear her eyes. "I will."

"Will you? Will you be the first?"

Lily's eyes traveled back to the snow. Her spirit began to calm, and with the relaxation came sedation. Exhaustion tunneled her vision. She put her palms against her thighs and leaned forward. Aurora's shoulder caught her hairline as she plowed against her. She felt Aurora falter and bend backward, yet the two of them stayed upright. Aurora did not put her hands on her, yet she did not push her away.

The two of them stayed like that for a long while, frozen in the snow, their hair brushed back by the frigid winds. Lily stared down at Aurora's legs. Lily buried her face deeper into her shoulder. She began to hum before she began to sing.

The two of them swayed together. The vibrations from Lily's throat bounced off Aurora's body. She could feel Aurora disappearing, her body becoming looser and watery. She moved to grip Aurora's sleeve.

"Hovan, Hovan Gorry og O

Gorry og, O, Gorry og O

Hovan, Hovan Gorry og O

I never found my baby, O…"

Lily had forgotten. It would always be unforgivable.

Aurora rested her cheek against Lily's hair. Lily pressed herself closer to her. When the sun's eyes shone over the horizon, Aurora would be a pile of bones. She would be mingled with the dead grass, sprouting up from the dirt.

The hours of the night passed slowly, in heavy clumps. Slumber merged with a dewy trance. The fatigue of mourning had left her soul stripped. From behind her eyelids, the blue-black night slowly blended with blobs of pink. Sunrise. A chilled rush of wind spread through her cheeks, thin fingers that brushed across the side of her face.

Lily lifted her head away from the snow.

The snow's surface was already pooling over with water as the sun began to stake its claim on the sky. Lily's mind spun in a dizzy smog. She raked her hands through her hair, trying to smooth out the tangles and angled her gaze upward. Her mouth felt dry, there was a sour aftertaste of something she was unable to place. Her legs burned as she stood. She looked up to the branch where Aurora had hung herself. Already, her face was evaporating from Lily's memory.

How long had she hung from that tree? How long had the police and their hounds searched for her before they realized it was a relief to forget? An unmarked pile of dirt was a satisfactory grave in their minds. She had not asked if Aurora regretted it, she had not even thought to ask. The woods were silent, save for the occasional far-off rustle of deer and squirrels. A person would never know that Aurora had ever been there. A person would never know that a world even existed outside of the forest. Existence began and ended there, in that place.

Supernova and an endless black hole.

"Lily," a voice called out in a desperate scream. "Lily, dear?"

The Doctor.

She knew that she could stay with Aurora, their souls floated through trees and slept in shadow together. She had to make the decision right then, right there. There was a time when Lily would have wished for that. She would have begged for it. Why was she not begging?

"Lily, your sister is desperately worried about you. I do think this is quite an unfortunate step backward."

She looked up at the sky again. She knew that the stars were there, but their light was hidden from her behind the all-consuming sunshine. She had been created. She was created. She existed. But the trees' branches consumed the starlight and the sunshine for themselves.

"I'm here," she said.

Did she want to exist?

"Lily? Keep talking, I'll follow your voice."

Had she been happy?

"I'm here, Doctor."

"I hear you."

"I'm here."

Slowly, the frantic pace of his footsteps neared her. She waited, not turning around. She refused to give the trees that satisfaction.

"Lily, Lily," The Doctor panted. "Oh, thank God."

The top of his balding head glistened with sweat, the shirt fabric under his armpits was moist. He was still in his flannel pajama pants, with boots haphazardly laced up around his ankles.

"I'm here," Lily said.

He laughed, breathless. "Yes. My, oh, my. You certainly are."

She crossed her arms, all at once railing against the urge to wrap them around his torso and hide her face in the crook of his neck. "You just now noticed that I was gone."

"Now, Lily, you know that I considered you responsible enough not to get bed checks."

"I thought I was free to leave any time I wanted."

"Come now. Our only goal is to get you well again."

"I don't want meds. Not your meds."

"But you want to get better?"

"I want to be different."

"Then, really, what's so bad about medication?"

She bit the inside of her cheek. "Because I didn't choose it. I just want to be a part of it. Couldn't we talk about it all?"

He laughed heartily at that. "You don't know anything about medications, not a thing. That's why I'm the doctor and you're the patient."

"Give me time, let me look them up. I don't want to be so drugged that I don't know where I am, or who I am."

"That is a sign of progress, indeed."

Lily watched him for a moment. "You don't see me, do you?"

He lowered his glasses down playfully. "Well, now I can't."

She took a step back. The only reason he came looking for her was because losing track of her again was to lose his reputation. He was a man of profound influence. She had known nothing of Meadowlark before coming there, and yet she immediately felt the radiation of The Doctor's pride. It would be his downfall, his greatest shame if Lily had been lost to the forest, if she had become another pile of bones dangling from a moth-bitten rope.

"I think someone died here," she said.

The Doctor's face sobered. He pushed his glasses against the bridge of his nose. "What?"

"Didn't Aurora Marnie disappear in the forest?"

"Well, that was many, many years ago. Long before you were alive, or I ever began working at Meadowlark. Before 'Meadowlark' was even 'Meadowlark', in fact."

Lily glanced over her shoulder. "I found bones at the base of that tree."

She watched as a visible shiver traveled through The Doctor's flesh.

"What?"

She sighed, staring at the top of his head. She calmed. "I think someone died here."

Chapter 12
The Present, Ending

"After more than three decades, the remains of twenty-five-year-old Aurora Marnie have been found." The reporter seemed to stare directly at Lily through the screen. "Marnie was a patient at the infamous Ivy-House mental facility, known to the world now as the renowned Meadowlark House. Marnie's remains have been returned to her family. Those in authority at Meadowlark have, thus far, refused to comment - despite multiple interview requests. At the present moment, it is unclear how the body was discovered, only that…"

"Oh, ho, ho," The Doctor snatched the remote from Lily's hand and switched the television back to *The Wizard of Oz*. "I've told you, dear, that is not the kind of thing we need to be seeing at this time."

She looked down at the curved mold of her fingers, still clutching the nonexistent television controller. "I don't feel right."

"Well, it's the medication, dear. It takes some getting used to, and I won't deny that what you've been given is very strong."

She blinked, rehydrating her eyes. The motion took eons. Stars were born and died in that time.

"Where's Seraphina? Why hasn't she come for our ride?" she asked. "She was supposed to be here days ago."

"You know, I'm sure that Seraphina lives quite a ways away in the mountains. She doesn't have a phone, only a radio. We've contacted her multiple times, but she always seems to be busy. But I've no doubt she'll come back soon enough."

Lily lifted her arm, the limb felt like a pound of lead. "She doesn't love me. She isn't ready. Not yet."

The Doctor looked to Nurse Kathy, who loomed in the doorway. "What's happening to her?"

Lily rubbed her lips together, the wounds there open and sore. "God, I'm so tired."

Nurse Kathy's heels clicked against the tiled floor, nearing her. "She doesn't appear to be responding terribly well, Doctor. Should we lower the dosage?"

Lily looked out the window. "I can feel him, can't you hear him running? I'm weak, and he knows it. He wants to find me and eat me while he can. While I'm too tired to fight back."

The Doctor stroked the edges of his jawbone. "Mark that down, what she just said."

"Yes, Doctor."

Lily's head dangled loosely at her left side. She curled her ankles inward. The depth of her vision distorted and her ears rang. "I'm dreaming, aren't I? Nothing about this feels real."

"Interesting," the Doctor said.

"What should we do?" Nurse Kathy tapped her pen against her clipboard.

"I daresay we ought to wait. I have a session with her later this afternoon. I'll examine her more closely at that time. Thank you, Nurse Kathy."

"Of course, Doctor."

Lily's temples burned, pain seared in flashes through her head. Her palms were moist with sweat. Her left arm ached. She was unable to recall how she had reached the chair. She could hardly remember anything from the past few days. She stared up at the yellowed image of Judy Garland.

"Let's allow her some space, yes? It's a process, you know." The Doctor told Nurse Kathy.

"What about Poe? Should we allow them to see one another again?"

Lily's lips parted. Only at that moment did she realize that she had not seen Poe since Christmas. They had allowed themselves to be caged, and neither had fought back.

"I think so. Poe is checking out today, of course. It might be therapeutic for them to say goodbye."

Tears welled-up in Lily's eyes. She swallowed, her throat clogged and wet. She ducked her head. Her hair no longer had the length or weight to curtain over her face. For the first time, her skin cried out for the sharp warmth of the chicken farm by the old highway. She wanted to rip off her shoes and feel the crunch of the golden, dead grass on the pads of her feet. The memory of the metal slide her father had installed in their backward, the way it burned her thighs as she traveled down it on hot summer afternoons, seeped through her brain. The days were quiet, the sun seared any humidity from the air. Blackbirds, silence, dust, the chickens clucking quietly in their coops. The sterility of Meadowlark was starting to make her queasy. Sunshine could not break through those walls. They were too thick and too white.

"I'll go fetch Poe. He should be packing his bags."

"Yes, quiet. Thank you, Nurse Kathy."

Lily's neck craned upward, and she stared up at the white ceiling. The lack of color infected her vision and overwhelmed her eyes.

"Lily?" The Doctor bent down to fix his eyes on the side of her face. "Dear, we're bringing Poe in to see you. A friend of his is coming to pick him up today. He's quite adamant that he does not wish to stay."

"Why wouldn't you let us see each other until now?"

"We were concerned, after what happened on Christmas. We felt that you were holding each other back from advancing your progress here."

Lily, for the first time since her mind had been flooded with medication, felt the tremors of rage within her. "I want to go with him."

"We can't allow that, dear."

"You told me I could leave, whenever I wanted. That's what you told me."

"Yes. Well, at the time, that was true. Since then, we've started to wonder if you might be a danger to yourself if we let you go now. Perhaps even a danger to others."

She mashed her teeth against one another. "Don't ever call me 'dear' again, never again, never." She slapped away a tear as it trailed down her cheek.

The Doctor shifted beside her. "Yes. I see. Well, that's that, then."

Lily heard steps in the space beside her.

"Seriously?" Poe's baritone voice permeated the room. "Just now? Right as I'm leaving, you let me out of solitary confinement?"

"That's a tad dramatic to say, don't you think?" The Doctor said.

Poe folded his arms across his chest. He sighed through his nose. "I could sue you, I could. Can you imagine? Can you imagine a lawsuit right on the heels of finding a dead girl from 30 years ago? The media are already shitting on you, and believe me, I can make it so terribly much worse. Do you reckon that's what you want?"

Lily's gaze shifted back to The Doctor. She wondered if the two of them were even aware that she was there.

The Doctor clenched and unclenched his fist. "I think you know that everything I've done here has been for your own good."

Poe lifted his eyebrows. "Really? How dare you?"

"Mr. Beckett, if it were up to me, I would not even allow you to leave here."

"Well, thank God it isn't your choice." Poe narrowed his eyes. "Fuck, this has been such a waste of time."

The Doctor's eyes cut down to look at Lily. "I see. Alright. Well, I have appointments and such, so perhaps I ought to leave the two of you alone to say goodbye."

Lily saw Poe's jaw clench. "What a privilege."

The Doctor laced his fingers in front of his stomach before leaving.

Once he had gone, Poe sat on the arm of the chair beside her's.

"Hey, Lily," he said. "I'm glad I get to see you before I go."

She pinched the skin on the palm of her hand. She barely felt the sensation. "Your boyfriend is coming for you? Coming to get you?"

"They called him on Christmas when they couldn't find us. He's my emergency contact. He's flown down. I can't stay here anymore, Lily. I'm sorry, I just can't."

"They won't let me out," Lily said.

"It'll be a few weeks more, maybe less. They want to make a point."

"And they don't want to make a point with you?"

"They're too afraid I'll do something to fuck them over if I stay. They've done all they can with me, anyway. Meds, group, sessions - there's nothing more they know how to do."

She looked down at her lap. The muscles of her legs that ballet had chiseled into marble were all but atrophied. "Do you feel any better? Any less crazy?"

He leaned forward on his elbows. "Christ, what have they got you on?"

"Do you feel any less crazy?"

He wore a black wool sweater and fitted jeans. His curls were gelled and styled back. In such a short time, he had grown so much older.

"I don't know. Maybe a little."

He was handsome, calm, surrendered to the world and his place in it. She combed her fingers through her hair. "I'm sorry I didn't know who you were when we met."

Poe pulled his body back and away from her. "Lily, come on."

"I don't know if I want you to forget about me. Do you think you will?"

"Lily," he said. "You're kidding yourself and I can't understand why. You're drowning but you won't let anyone help you. How in the shit do you expect to get any better? I'm not saying you have to do it here, but you have to make a choice."

A chill traveled through her shoulders and back. "You don't know anything about me."

"You can't live like this. Of course I understand. Don't you know I understand?"

"I don't."

He lifted his palms, holding them out to her. "Just work with me. Please, that wall is so thick I can barely see you. I'm trying to get to you, why won't you help me?"

Lily paused. Her breathing got heavier. She stared at him for a moment. "I don't know how to say it. I never make sense when I talk."

"God, Lily," he groaned.

"I'm fine, I promise. I'm just tired. I'm glad your boyfriend's coming, I'm happy you're doing better. I mean that. I'm serious."

He covered his eyes with his hands. "Christ."

"I'm happy for you, Poe. I want you to be happy. Thank you for trying."

He scrubbed his hand over his face. His eyes were reddened and wet, his voice trembled a little. "Can I hug you? Or shake your hand?"

He rose on his feet and stepped forward. He placed his palm over her's as it laid flat on the couch arm. He sniffled as he moved to press his lips softly into her hairline. The room was quiet. He was warm beside her. She felt him shake gently with light sobs before pulling away from her.

"God, I'm so sorry," he said waveringly, his voice burned with tears. "I wish I could help you, but I don't know how."

"It's ok," she said, and then she smiled. She rubbed her numb hand over his shoulder.

"Try to answer the phone when I call, if you can."

"Poe?" Nurse Kathy's sickly-sweet voice questioned behind them. "Poe, dear, a Mr. Shepard Phillips has come to pick you up."

Lily caught his gaze at the moment when real light beamed into his eyes for the first time since she had met him. A young man stepped out of the hall and into the common room. He was lovely, with thick brown hair and lightly tanned skin. Eyes as green and lush as a forest. She could see how Poe would fall in love with him.

"Shepard?" Poe's tone was tender.

Shepard's face crumbled. He let out a watery laugh. "I think so."

Poe pressed his palm into his chest. "Oh, God."

He lunged at Shepard and threw his arms around his neck. Shepard's arms twisted through Poe's torso and he pressed his lips into the burrow of Poe's shoulder.

Lily could not hear what they said.

Poe intertwined his fingers through Shepard's hair. Lily turned away. She could not imagine being loved like that.

She stood. Her legs went watery as she slunk into the shadows of the hallway. She watched as the two of them stayed locked together. It seemed impossible that even an atom of air could have existed between them. Nausea overtook her. Dizziness swallowed her depth perception. She slumped down, her knees buckled as she dropped to the tile. Her lips flapped open, her head felt all too heavy for her neck to support. Consciousness slipped away from her, moments of black pushed her into nothing. She was unsure how long she sat there.

"Lily? My, my, what are you doing down there?"

Her weighted eyelids dragged open as she tipped her head up. She stared at the blurred image of The Doctor.

"What?" she slurred.

The Doctor clasped his hands together. "What are you doing down there? Are you feeling alright?"

Her limbs tingled. "What? I was tired."

"It happens to the best of us. Shall we stand up? I daresay it's a tad early for your session, but I finished my work faster than expected."

"I've got to get out of here."

The Doctor reached down to pull her upward by her elbow. "You're being a little silly, don't you think?"

She stumbled as she was taken toward The Doctor's office. "I need to go outside, just for a minute."

"That sounds quite nice, indeed. In fact, I have a bit of a surprise for you. I think Seraphina is riding down from the mountain for a ride later today."

She began to pant. "I can't see her today, I…"

The Doctor slowed his pace slightly. "I beg your pardon?"

"I don't feel right. Tell her not to come."

"It's quite too late for that. Remember, she doesn't have a phone. I can't get in contact with her now."

Her eyes fluttered shut. "You're going to kill me."

"It was my understanding that you and Seraphina got along well."

"I'm not ready. Neither of us are ready. We don't love each other like Shepard and Poe."

"What's changed? This is very discouraging."

Lily's eyes flashed up to him again. "You don't know how to see me. You're killing me."

He again towed her toward his office. "You'll feel better after our hypnotherapy session. I admit I've been a little disappointed, our more recent sessions haven't yielded the same results as our early ones."

"I'm getting out of here. I'm leaving."

"I'm hoping that a new method will get us back to where we were before."

"You're not listening. I won't be here soon. You didn't listen to Aurora, either."

"Now watch this step, don't trip."

Lily lifted her foot and placed it on the carpet of The Doctor's office floor. "I'm going. Do you understand?"

The Doctor gestured to her usual chair. The image bent and swayed before her eyes. "Go ahead and sit down. And we'll get started, yes?"

"No," she said.

"Go ahead and sit down," he said. "And close your eyes, relax, and listen to the sound of my voice."

Light flares of irritation sparked up in Lily's stomach, but not fire. She leaned her weight against the arm of the couch, rising to her feet. "No. I need to decide something."

"Oh? What does that mean, precisely?"

She panted heavily. "I'm not going under hypnosis again. It isn't working, I won't do it anymore."

The Doctor stared at her for a moment. "Yes. I see. This puts quite a wrench in the process, hypnotherapy only works if you want it to work. Perhaps we can simply talk."

She lifted her hand up to her hair. It was creased with soft waves, falling just to the top of her shoulders. "You can't help me. Maybe someone can, but not you."

"I could if you'd allow me to."

She attempted to steady herself as she kept her gaze on him, unbroken. "No."

"And why is that?"

His voice was devoid of emotion.

She flung her hands out in front of her. "Because you aren't listening. You're crazy. You're as crazy as I am."

His face sagged. He folded his arms over his chest. "Of course. Of course."

"Do you even hear yourself? God, I can't stand it anymore."

"What can't you stand?" he replied, tranquil and serene.

Her chest heaved in and out as she stammered, "This."

"And are you saying there's nothing wrong with you?"

Her body froze-over in a glacier. Her fingertips numbed as the air grew heavy. "What?"

The Doctor tilted his chin up at her. "I wasn't surprised when I saw you talking with Poe for the first time, I wasn't surprised that the two of you got along. The both of you have similar problems, more similar than you'd think."

"Don't say anything bad about him."

"The two of you share something, and it's not right. It's toxic."

Lily's throat iced, the saliva freezing over. "I…"

"You are both desperate for control, both of you want to control *something*. Anything. Poe wanted control over the world around him, you want to control yourself. Neither of you will ever get what you want. And neither of you can accept it."

"You don't know anything about me," she replied, working to keep her voice steady.

"You can't stand that you have to live in that head of yours," he said. "Everything you do is a form of protest against yourself. But you can never decide what exactly you want out of it all. You ask too much, and you give too little. Your career as a ballerina wasn't what brought you here. It's an excuse, it's your crutch."

She balled her hands into a fist. "I know I'm not…a…"

"'Not 'a' what? Say it."

Her eyes pooled over with tears. "I'm not a dancer anymore."

"No. You're not."

Her eyes flickered down to The Doctor's feet. "I'm not a ballerina anymore."

He continued moving forward. "Have you just now woken up?"

She bit down on the inside of her cheek. "I'll be ugly for the rest of my life."

"Why did you try to kill yourself after your performance of *The Firebird*?"

"What?"

"Why did you try to kill yourself on December 3rd?"

"I…"

"What is your obsession with ballet? What do you think it'll solve for you?"

She began to tremble, her heart palpitated furiously in her chest. "It's all I have."

"It's all you *had*."

She winced as though he had stabbed her. "God."

"Can you tell me what ballet is for you? Do you even know?"

Lily's eyes cut over to him. "I was beautiful when I danced."

He lifted his palm up. "Every ballerina is beautiful. Why were you so special?"

She breathed in hard through her nose, blood rushed to her brain and blurred her vision. "I wasn't 'special', I was…it was the only thing I was good at. I don't know how to do anything else. But I wasn't 'special'."

She stared at the empty space on the wall where *Bedroom in Arles* once hung. The Doctor shuffled to move behind her. "What's the point in lying now? Why not simply be honest? What have you got left to lose?"

She wished there was a window so she could see the outside. "I'm telling you the truth."

"See, this is your problem, Lily. Have you ever read Lacan?"

"You know I don't know what that is."

"His best essay was by far *The Mirror Stage*, it's all about self-image," he said. "Everyone constructs a perfect version of themselves, which is inevitably impossible to live up to."

"I want to go back to my room."

"According to Lacan, no matter how desperately one desires to become that absolute version of themselves, they never can. Indeed, to become one's ideal self would render them totally psychotic, or an undeveloped fetus," he said.

She kept her arms crossed, pressing them into her ribs until they ached. "Which one am I? The psychotic or the undeveloped fetus?"

The Doctor's face remained steely. "Who is your ideal-self? Can you describe her for me?"

"I want to go back to my room."

"In our hypnotherapy sessions, you consistently talked about something called, 'the Beast.' Do you remember this? Do you know what you were talking about when you said that?"

She felt the blood drain from her face and drip into her feet. "No. No. Just rambling."

"I think the Beast is you. I think the Beast is the part of you that keeps hurting people, that keeps hurting yourself."

She stared at him. "The Beast is real. He's a demon, he possesses me. He's a parasite, he isn't me. I'd do anything to kill him."

The Doctor bent his head from left to right. "You enjoyed ballet, yes? Enjoyed it very much. You were so devoted, I'd venture to guess, that you danced constantly. It was your reprieve. It was all you did. You never had a spare moment. Your diet, your free-time, your entire existence was devoted to dance."

She relaxed for a moment. "I was passionate. I told you, it was the only talent I had."

"Yes. Passionate because it fended off the Beast, didn't it?"

"The Beast couldn't get me when I was on stage, when I was performing. It was the one time I knew I was safe. It was the one time he couldn't make me ugly."

The Doctor paced about the room. "Your ideal-self was whomever you were when you danced for an audience, is that right?"

She grew flustered again as moths nibbled on her brain. "I was a ballerina, that's all I was. But I wasn't great. I wouldn't even have made principle anywhere else except that tiny theater."

"But you *were* a principal, weren't you? I daresay you were *the* principal."

"Only for one season."

"But for that one season, you were better, weren't you? You were better than everyone else, and you knew it. That's why you got to be the Firebird. If I don't miss my guess, you weren't the most refined, but you were real. You were raw; that's what they told you."

"Who told you that?"

He laughed loudly, so loudly that she flinched. "No one told me, dear. You're textbook, you're not the rarified creature you'd like to imagine you are."

Lily imagined ripping her fingernails across his throat until blood fountained from his neck. "I never said that I was."

"You hardly had to," he said. "Don't you think I see you? All it took was one look from me and I knew you."

"You don't know anything."

"I know that you're a schizophrenic with severe anxiety and intermittent explosive disorder. That's exactly what you are."

"I want to go back to my room."

"You know," he continued, throwing his full weight toward her. "I have a theory about you. I think you tried to kill yourself on December 3rd because you couldn't imagine a world where you weren't the star."

"That's isn't —"

"And you tried to kill yourself after *The Firebird* because you realize you weren't the center of attention anymore."

"I'm not —"

"You were beautiful when other people were looking at you. That's what you wanted back."

"You don't understand."

He kept his gaze on her, he never looked away. "You're a childish, selfish, maddening little diva who can't stand not being the prima ballerina you thought you were. Reality has thrust you headfirst into the real world and you can't cope. When your sad little attempts to exit it didn't work, you came here. You came here to exist in a place where you don't have to really exist. Because that's what you want. You can't admit that you are average. You will live an average life and die an average death. You'll never be a famous dancer at the New York City Ballet. You are screaming into a void, no one can hear you and no one wants to. And it all goes back to December 3rd. It all goes back to when you —"

"I tried to kill myself because I'm ugly." She screamed. Her face seared with red heat. "I was beautiful when I was The Firebird because at that moment, on that stage, the only thing that existed in me was perfect and magical, and nothing evil could reach me. It couldn't reach me up on that stage. I made that audience believe I was something beautiful, it wasn't real, but I felt beautiful. I wasn't an angel, I wasn't a monster, I was something else and I felt like I could live in my skin for a little while. I was free."

She had not felt the tears that trickled down her cheeks until her words had ceased. She breathed heavily. Her hands trembled at her sides. A thick layer of dead skin had peeled from her body, leaving her raw and fresh, trembling in the cold daylight. She watched as The Doctor's deep frown contorted into a satisfied grin. He placed a hand on his stomach, leaning back as if satisfied from a hearty meal.

"My, oh, my. Good Heavens, what a catharsis that was. I feel as though we've hit a breakthrough in your process." He stepped forward, prompting her to move back. "You finally opened up to me, it's a wonderful step in the right direction."

"You're not even here," she whispered.

"You are truly a wonder," he said. "I'm going to make you better and turn you into any other woman walking down the street. I'll make you normal. You'll be able to find a man, you'll have babies, you'll live to a ripe old age and die in a rocking chair."

"You're not here. You're not listening to me."

He pulled her against him. "Take heart, my darling. Take heart. It's a process you know."

Something under Lily's skin squirmed as he kept his arms locked around her torso. What right did he have to touch her? What right did he have to call her his 'darling'? He did not want her, his interest in her extended only as far as crafting her into an unobtrusive lady who looked good on paper. His prescriptions would never correct her distraught brain chemistry, they would only sedate her into an anesthetized hush. He could not supply the medicine she needed.

Her fingers unfurled behind his back, extending out toward the lovely blue and white paperweight perched on his desk. Her fingertips cooled when she touched the chilled, cold, aloof object; impartial to its owner. It felt nothing for the man who it had served for so long.

The Doctor's breath was hot on the back of her neck. She pulled the paperweight to her slowly. The object made tiny scraping sounds as it snuck across his wooden desk until she had gained a firm hold on the paperweight. Her gaze moved to the back of his head and neck. Those seconds lasted for eons, until finally, she knew that she was ready.

Without alerting him, she carefully raised her arm.

He shifted slightly to adjust his grip on her.

She allowed her eyelids to fall shut, calming her breathing. In that moment of bittersweet silence, her arm swung down, and the paperweight made contact with The Doctor's head.

He cried out and released her. He stumbled backward, his eyes feral and wide. His lips flapped as he reached up to cradle his head. Lily watched as he looked down at the weapon in her hand. The paperweight, once his companion, had betrayed him. Terror and excitement flooded her as she backed away toward the open doorway. She could hardly believe how fast it had all happened.

"I've been attacked by a patient! I've been —"

Rage filled her to the brim and spilled over as she grunted and thrust the paperweight to the ground. It shattered. Before she had a chance to consider, she turned on her heels and sprinted down the hall. She heard The Doctor's screams fade as she tore through the facility. She heard Nurse Kathy calling out orders. She felt as though she was flying as she rushed through Meadowlark, the sterilized white blinded her.

She did not look back as she ran. She had no idea who chased her, or if she was being chased at all. The halls smeared into a mess of white and Van Gogh. Within the maze, finally she reached the doorway. The nurse guarding the station looked up at her from her glasses. Lily screeched to a halt.

"Where are you going in such a hurry?"

Lily panted vigorously. She heard clacking footsteps rapidly approach. The exuberance at her approaching freedom was diluted with dread at being recaptured.

She looked back to the nurse. "I need you to open the door."

"I've heard that there's a violent patient on the loose. It would be quite the irresponsible action to open the door and let that violent patient out into the public."

"Open the fucking door."

"I'm not sure it's appropriate to swear as such."

Lily clenched her fist, then threw her body toward the nurse's desk. She jumped back with her hands clenching the arms of her chair. Lily scanned the painted white desk and saw a neon red button risen on the surface. She slammed her hand down on it, and the door clicked, unlocking. She was through the door and out of the building before the nurse could stop her.

Her sneakers merged with the icy ground. Her lungs chilled as they met with the cold air. She sped into the forest. The sun was setting, cradled by the horizon. The sky was colored with bright hues of purple and silver. Despite the weather, she felt herself burn within her own skin. It seemed as though forever had passed since she had truly looked at the sky.

As she ran, her skin began to stretch and contort. Everything fell away while she sprinted. The sky lost its vibrancy of violets and grays and became awash in a limitless abyss of black. The lush greens of the woods dulled to a gentler shade from the frost, then thawed into a harsh white.

Her fingernails broke away from her flesh, falling from her as she ran. Her skin ripped open, blood spewed out and onto the white ground. Her hair collapsed in blonde clumps. A thick, silky hide took the place of her previous membrane. Heavy hooves metamorphosed from her hands and feet. She buckled down, raced against the fading sunset light on all fours. Two bone-white antlers sprouted from her head, flowering up to the sky.

Rushing through the forest, a taste of biting wind shot through her tongue. Freedom, she was so close to feeling true and genuine freedom. Yet, she was too wild to feel that freedom. Breath came out in hot puffs through her snout. As she began to dissipate into the woods, she caught sight of something up ahead. It bounded forward, moving up towards the blurred horizon. Her ears perked up.

In that immense space before her, she saw another white stag. Its antlers and eyes were a stony black, pure ebony against absolute pearl. Cool, smoothed marble. Its chest was ripped open in a bright red gash. Its heart was exposed and beating briskly within the open wound. The pain must have been unimaginable. Lily knew who it was. She sprinted harder, her body burned from the speed. She felt death strangle her as she went, yet she refused to allow herself to stop.

She chased the white stag for what felt like eons and sprinted through what she thought were miles of woodland. She loved the white stag. Its spirit calmed her, connected her to an invisible world. Its spirit had existed ever since the universe had split into creation, just as her soul had been, just as every soul had been. The spirit of the white stag was a medium. The white stag linked souls to the everlasting world, which was born and had died a multitude of times. The white stag lived someplace between these two dimensions. The white stag transported Lily to that plane.

The bond between them had begun to wither as she had grown older. She was too far gone to know the white stag or live in the white stag's world. Lily panted in her pursuit. The white stag blended with the ground and sky. Lily fell behind. She tried to run faster, her body crumpled under the pressure of her sprint. Her legs stumbled beneath her, but still, she pursued. Without realizing it, her fur had reverted to dry, pale skin. Her scalp burned as the hair regrew, coming down in a wavy, thick mass that ended just past her shoulders. She was pulled upright to continue on two legs instead of four. Her torso shrunk. Her fingers stretched out and extended, curling into a fist.

She heard herself breathing heavily. Her limbs flared with blistering pain. Saliva fell from her mouth and off her lower lip. Curls of darkness gathered around the edges of her eyes from the lack of oxygen reaching her brain. She extended her arm out toward the white stag. The grass and trees materialized again, brightening the land with green and white frost. The sky was suddenly colored with the deep bluish-black of night, and in that infinite space, stars glittered a flickering silver.

Lily grasped the white stag's antlers to slow herself and ensure that the white stag could not escape. Her lungs felt as though they would burst as she swiveled the white stag's head, forcing their eyes to connect. Little droplets of sweat from her palms ran in rivers down the white stag's antlers. Her knees and legs caved in and she toppled to the ground. The white stag stared at her. Its gaping chest wound still leaked blood. Yet, he seemed utterly calm.

Lily shook her head. "Why did you do this to me?" she asked, breathless.

The white stag stared at her, unblinking.

Lily tightened her grip on its antlers. "I know you can hear me. I know you know me. Don't you remember how much I loved you? I would have done anything for you."

Clouds of breath flowed from the white stag's snout.

Lily pushed her forehead into the white stag's. "I thought you loved me. I was tied to you. You were my hope, and then you left. You abandoned me in that bathtub. You *know* you did."

He pressed himself closer to Lily, his hooves lifted and then fell back down to the ground.

"I want an answer. I know you can hear me. You made me like this, and then you left me. How could you do that? Why would you do that?"

The white stag attempted to back out of her grip.

Lily's handle on its antlers solidified. "I'm not losing you again."

The white stag twisted his head, and Lily's grip was wrestled away from her. She cried out, falling to the ground. She looked up to the white stag, her palms flat against the ground, crunching down into the ice.

"You let me know what it felt like to be beautiful, and then you made me ugly."

The white stag tilted its head to the side.

Lily's spirit shuddered to an eerie calm. "I was created from cells in the ocean, formed through millions upon millions of years of evolution. Stars died for me. All those people who came before me, all that time. There must be a reason."

The white stag pawed at the ground, snorting gently.

Lily swiped her tongue over her cracked lips. "I know you decided it would be this way. I blame you."

It stared at her for a moment, the exposed heart pumped steadily. It bent its legs, and the lean, long body folded to the ground.

Lily reached out her quaking hand, her fingertips barely brushed up against its fur.

"Just help me understand. I want to know you again. I need to know that I'm not a failed experiment. I need to know that there's a purpose to all of this."

Lily rested her palm between his eyes and snout.

"What are you trying to say?" she asked in a whisper. "Are you blaming *me*?"

The white stag sighed again.

"I would have gone anywhere, done anything for you to have stayed with me."

The white stag snorted softly.

Lily stared at the white stag. She shook her head gently. "I can't understand you anymore. I've forgotten the language and I don't remember how I learned it in the first place."

The white stag pressed deeper into her touch.

"What is that? I don't know what that means."

Its legs remained tucked underneath its sleek body. The blood from its exposed heart leaked onto the icy grass.

"Are you still waiting for me?"

A rustle came from the brush behind her. She gasped, flew upwards and placed her body between the noise and the white stag. Without even seeing him, she knew who it was. She flipped her head back toward the white stag.

"Go," she commanded.

The white stag stood up slowly, watching her.

"I need you to leave. I won't have you hurt by him."

The white stag pawed at the ground, snorting once more.

"I'll find you again, one day. Just go. When I'm ready, I'll find you again."

The white stag turned away with some reluctance before galloping off and back into the woods. Lily kept her eyes fixed on the creature for as long as she could, until it had moved too deeply into the forest to remain within her line of vision. The moment the white stag disappeared, rage swept over her like a tidal wave. She whipped her head back around to stare at the noise.

"Why did you have to come now?"

A low growl radiated from the shadow, and a hulking figure emerged. His paws were rooted firmly into the ground. His back arched upward. His teeth bared in a snarl. He had selected his moment well, and he knew it. Lily's fingers rolled up into fists.

"I hate you," she growled in a low, deep voice.

The Beast snapped at her. His ears were pressed to the back of his head.

Lily forced herself to move forward. "I hate that you live inside me. I hate how you feed off me."

The Beast lunged toward her, opening and closing its jaw rapidly.

"What do you think will happen if you kill me?" she shouted. "You can't live without me. The moment I die, so will you. Don't you understand that?"

The Beast paused, slightly lowering his body to the ground.

"Is that all you are? A parasite. Is that all you have? You can't rest until you've destroyed both of us."

He curled his lips back over his teeth.

Lily's heart pounded furiously in her chest. "You want to die, don't you? You need us both to end so you can find peace."

The Beast's eyes softened for a moment.

Lily's hatred and fear remained solidified, but she continued to move closer to the Beast.

"All you want is rest," she said in a hoarse whisper.

The Beast suddenly launched himself at her, his paws beating into the ground. Lily stiffened, refusing to flinch at his advance.

He stopped short of her.

They stared into one another's eyes, the same shade of blue, mere inches apart. His breath was hot against her face.

"You had so many chances. You could have done it so many times. The night after *The Firebird*, a few more pills that you'd have had me. December 3rd, December 3rd would have been perfect."

The Beast made a noise that existed somewhere between a roar and a bark.

"If you'd made me swallow a few more pills, it would have worked. And in that bathtub, if I'd have cut a little deeper into my wrists, I would have bled so much faster. They wouldn't have been able to save me at the hospital."

He threw his head over his shoulder and lowered his tail.

"Why didn't you do it?"

The Beast growled again. The noise rumbled through his throat.

Lily wanted to touch him. She did not. "I begged for it once. All I thought I wanted was to not 'be' anymore. I didn't think I deserved to be alive because of the things I'd done, all the things I was afraid I'd do."

The Beast's snarl died down. He watched her.

Lily was desperate to lay her hands against his hide. She did not. She had always wanted to know what he felt like. "I don't know what I deserve anymore. I don't know what'll happen to me, if I'll be happy, if my life will do more bad than good. I don't know if I even matter, at all. I don't have the answers."

He huffed air through his nose. His eyes darted over her face wildly.

"Not now. You've missed your chance," she said.

The Beast growled, displaying his teeth again.

"Not today. Not right now. No. I don't know why, but not today."
He barked and snapped at her.

Lily backed away slowly.

"Today I want to exist. That's my choice, that's my decision."

The Beast began to pace back and forth, twitching erratically.

She looked the Beast in his eyes and said, "I choose to exist."

The Beast let loose a deep scream that echoed through the forest. Lily bent her fingers into claws and dragged them across his shoulder blade. He cried out, fixed his infuriated blue eyes into her's.

"Lily," screamed a voice from a short distance away.

Beams from flashlights broke through the darkness. Her head snapped away from the Beast. She was blinded momentarily from gazing directly into the light.

"Lily," the voice called again.

She put her hand up against the brightness.

"What are you doing out here?" the voice asked.

Lily suddenly recognized it as Seraphina and lowered her hand. "I'm here."

"You could've killed him, you know, you could've killed that doctor," Seraphina gasped, frantic.

She spun around, looking to where the Beast had been. Where he once stood, there was merely a bundle of tall brush and shrubbery, crystallized over with ice.

Seraphina dismounted Pharaoh and aimed the flashlight to the ground. She shouted over her shoulder, "I found her! She's over here."

Other voices answered in a mass, too tangled for Lily to understand.

Lily stared at Seraphina for a moment before asking, "What are you doing here?"

"Your doctor's alright, if you care," Seraphina replied. She kept one fist on Pharaoh's reins. "And he doesn't want to press charges, he just wants you back."

Lily didn't move, not even a step. "I had to get out. I had to get out of there."

"You scared the living hell out of everyone. There's got to be at least fifteen people out looking for you. They called the police, I'm pretty sure some news people are coming."

"I don't love you, not yet."

Seraphina looked off into the cold darkness of night as though she had not heard her. "I can't do this, Lily. I have no idea how to do this. I don't understand you. I don't understand this."

Lily's eyelids fluttered with the weight of the tears beneath them. She swallowed a painful wad of saliva. "I know. It isn't our time yet."

Seraphina looked at her, brow furrowed. "What does that mean?"

"I don't know," Lily said. "I don't know."

She sighed. "I'm not trying to hurt you. I want you to come back to Meadowlark. I need you safe."

Lily tried to smile. "I had to go. I had to get out. And I've decided."

Seraphina was quiet for a moment, then shook her head. "I can't give you what you want. Do you even know what you want?"

Lily refused to move closer to Seraphina. "Tonight, I think so."

The voices and pounding footsteps grew more prominent. Orders were called out, and in that confusion, she heard a man shout, "She's this way. Remember, we can't have her bloody. The media are already here with cameras, she *cannot* have visible wounds."

Lily's breath became shallow as she sucked in air through her dry, cracked lips. "Are these people out here afraid of me?"

"I think so."

Men dressed in dark clothes melted against the background of the night, moving in a tight circle toward her.

"Target in-sight, I see her."

"Get the tranquilizer ready."

"Is she armed?"

"Negative, not armed, but possibly aggressive. Be prepared to use force but be careful. Stay clear of her face."

Lily kept her gaze fixed on Seraphina. She knew it would be the last time she would see her for a long while. Perhaps forever. Her heart felt as though it would burst inside her chest from beating so vigorously. "Do you think I can find it?"

"Find what?"

The men continued their hysterical shouting, yet, as Lily stared at Seraphina, their voices collapsed around her, sinking into a soft murmur. The world turned very slowly around her. The wind danced through the trees. The earth sent undetectable tremors through the mountain. She existed. She felt every hair rise on her arms and legs. Her pillowy hair puffed up in a cloud of frizz behind her. It was only when she tilted her head to examine a growing sensation of pain that she noticed a gash on her shoulder. Her sweater had been sliced open.

When she was eight, she had broken Cynthia Gerard's arm. She had tormented Dan Clifton when she was ten; she was the reason he was still in therapy. By the time she was in middle school, every child who knew of her saw the Beast when they looked at her. They did their best to keep their distance from her wrath, and she made sure anyone who did not regretted their decision. Her mother had refused to let her cut her hair when she was twelve, so she had shattered a prized vase that had been given to her mother by Lily's grandfather. Her mother had wept while trying to clean up the ashes of the vase from the carpet. Her temper had been legendary at her high school. Her peers had been fascinated by the way her shy nature could unfold into such untamable rage within moments. Everyone always tiptoed around her, afraid of waking the dragon which lay sleeping inside her stomach.

When she was sixteen, a boy named Tristan had told her he had a crush on her. He had said it so loudly that the rest of their history class had heard him. Two weeks later, he had sobbed next to her on a bench in an empty park and had told her that he actually loved a boy named Christopher. She had placed her fingers over the top of his hand and smiled at him. She saw him again in the street a year and a half after graduation. Tristan had smiled when he saw her. He had pulled her into his arms and pressed his face into the crook of her neck. His face had reddened and his eyes had crystallized with tears when he had walked away.

To Seraphina, Lily had become a unicorn with a wild mane and a sharpened horn. That horn terrified her. She was afraid of it impaling her if she got too close. Unicorns are deadly if disrespected, if caged. Yet, Seraphina was too intrigued to back away, she wanted a closer look. She would always want a closer look.

To Poe, she was a confused bird who flew into windows at the sight of its own reflection. To The Doctor, she was a lovely psychotic who looked good in pictures, a madwoman in the attic who he could lead out of the darkness and down the stairs. Then one day, Hallelujah, at last she would be a madwoman in the living room. To her mother and her father and her sister, she was the ugly black sheep who they hoped would be snatched by a wolf. They had felt her wool. It was wiry and harsh against bare flesh.

She had become so much, all tied into a poorly wrapped pile of decaying flesh and bone. Her dancing had stirred something beautiful in people, in herself. Her combustible spirit and sharp tongue had made her ugly to the same audiences who had once watched her supernova for them on stage. She had cut her hair, and now she had no idea what she was.

"A shaved bear looks a lot like a person. Did I ever tell you that?" Seraphina said softly. "When they stand up on their hind legs, they almost seem human. Did you know that?"

A pair of hands grabbed Lily's wrists, and another dug into the soft places on her arms.

"What do you mean?" she asked. Her voice shook as she was jostled by the loud men.

"I don't know."

Lily smiled.

"Restrain her. Get her legs."

One of the men wrapped his hand around Lily's chin.

"Hey, hey, look at me," he commanded. "Do you know that you attacked a doctor?"

Lily's insides burned as a sudden fire ignited within her. For the first time in what felt like forever, she allowed herself to burn. She breathed heavily as her jaw parted. She snapped down on the fingers that dared to touch her. What gave him the right?

"Fuck! The bitch bit me," he cried. "Get her tranquilized."

"Don't hurt her. She didn't mean anything," Seraphina called out.

To the man, she was a bitch.

"Come on, what's taking so long?"

More men's cold hands grabbed her. She gathered a wad of saliva onto one side of her cheek, slid it down her tongue so it whipped out of her mouth and onto one of the men's faces. He went backward as though he had been shot. Some of the other men laughed.

One of them said, "That's more action from a girl than you've had in a long time, huh Nick?"

"She's a spirited little filly, I'll say that," Nick replied. He was laughing, too.

"Don't touch her," Seraphina yelled. "She'll calm down if you stop touching her."

The men ignored her.

"Are we allowed to do it?" One of the men asked.

"She attacked me," Nick said. "Everyone will understand. If those fuckers point their cameras at her when she does some shit like this, it'll —"

"I understand, sir."

Lily allowed the fire to drip into her veins. Her limbs flailed as she worked to free herself from the men's grip. She grunted through gritted teeth. Her hair tangled into knots as she flung her body around.

"Get that needle in her. Do it now.'

"Stop fighting, Lily. You're going to hurt yourself."

"Come on. Before she does anything else."

An angry sting in her arm worked through her flesh and into her blood. Within seconds, her mind slowed to a sluggish stillness. Her vision blurred. Her limbs lost their ferocity and grew loose. Her mouth tumbled open in a slack, a low moan escaped from her lips.

"Good job, boys. Let's get her back before she's gone completely. Keep her awake."

Lily heard Seraphina call out her name, and then she was silent. She lost her grip on consciousness. She dropped down to her knees, her head swiveled on her shoulders.

"Damn. Maybe it was a little too much."

Lily's gaze fell back as she looked up at the clouded sky. Her breathing was hard and lethargic as she stared at the soft, white light of the moon. The orb was obscured by misty, thick vapor.

To the Beast, she was the only thing he ever hungered for. His appetite would never extend beyond her. The searing pain in his belly would never silence or give him peace until he had made her his meal.

After a supernova, the only thing that remains was what was left of the star's center. The star's center then had two choices for what it could become, depending on its mass: a neutron star or a black hole. A neutron star could have an ocean, it could have an atmosphere. It continued to spin even after such an explosion. A neutron star was lovely in space, even in darkness. A black hole devoured everything in its wake. Nothing escaped a black hole, no matter. No light. It was epic, awesome, all-encompassing in its power. It was grand, but there could be nothing else. Nothing else except the black hole. There could be no light. The core could become one or the other, but it did not have the power to become both.

Lily stared at the moon. The clouds shifted until pale light was exposed.

"Keep her awake," one of the men said. "Don't let her pass out."

Lily knew that Seraphina watched from a distance. She almost thought that she could hear her breathing. Lily did not attempt to focus her eyes on Seraphina. She only stared up at the moon. She had never truly realized how vast the sky was. There was freedom in the sky.

"I'm a stag," she whispered.

The moon's light tunneled in, and her vision lost sight of everything until there was only darkness.

Chapter 13
The Dream

There was a great silence on the moon. The dust felt cold on my flesh. I sat on my heels with my legs tucked underneath myself. My hands rested against my thighs. My thumb traced over the soft fabric of my dress. I stared down at the Earth and watched as clouds swirled over its surface. The planet spun slowly. There were no mirrors on the moon. I did not have any idea what I looked like. I felt my crimped hair; lifted in a wave behind me. Three feathers dangled from the left side of my head. They were secured in a thin braid. I ran my fingers through them. One black, another grey, and the last white. They were smooth and felt like velvet. My gaze fell back down to the Earth. I wished I knew who watched. Could anyone see me up there?

My dress was made up of a fabric I had never felt before. It was delicate and supple, yet I had no fear about the bindings loosening and falling apart. I also had no memory of the dress before its presence on my body. Its blackness created a sharp contrast to the glowing paleness of the moon's surface. Tiny, sparkling jewels were encrusted into the cloth's edges. Around the waist - a thick, shimmering silver band secured the dress loosely to my hips. The dress was unfitted, it did not make any attempt to cling to my body.

A golden crown with deer antlers lay on the moon's surface, just to the side of my thigh. I plucked it up and scrubbed off the thin layer of dust that coated the flawless surface. I lifted it and secured it around my head. It had a heaviness that weighed my skull down. I knew it would not fall. My audience would never forgive such an infraction. I pressed my hands into my face. It was clean and free of any makeup. No powder, no strip lashes, no sticky red paint on my lips.

The Earth's colors were astonishing. It was easy to forget the beauty of the contrasting blues of the skies and oceans. Time moved differently there than it did on my planet. Everything felt so much faster, and somehow slower at the same time. It was lonely with the audience so far away. The sun served as my stage light. It was positioned a lifetime away from me. I rubbed my arms up and down, though I could not feel the cold of the moon or the heat from the friction I created. I read once that no atmosphere exists on the moon.

The beating of wings startled me. I flipped my head to the side. The feathers twisted into my hair fell back over my shoulder. Two massive white wings flew in from somewhere above. Without even seeing her face, I knew who the wings carried. I smiled.

Aurora was dressed in a long, silver gown. Her hair was decorated with an assortment of flowers and gems. She landed on a small asteroid which pushed itself lazily through the cosmos. She shook out her wings and smoothed her feathers. She ran her palms over the wrinkles in her dress. Our eyes met and mine began to water. She kept her gaze fixed on me before slowly allowing a gentle grin to rise through her face. I was not sure she would come.

Piano music suddenly piped in through the countless stars and worlds. It echoed through a vast nothingness. Beethoven's no. 5 piano concerto. Emperor. I stood up, arranged my body in fifth position to signal my readiness to begin. Aurora watched from her place on the floating rock. Her eyes brightened with what seemed to be pride. I tipped my head to whoever may be applauding back on Earth.

And then I began to dance.

I was not wearing pointe shoes. My ugly feet, bent and twisted with bunions and blisters, were on display for everyone to see.

I never was the Firebird. She only possessed me for a short while and allowed me to feel total detachment and freedom. That kind of power was new to me. She showed me a way of existence I had always wanted and never knew was possible. And then she left because that has always been her way. I had been foolish to think that I could catch her.

I danced without restriction or rules. I did not have choreography to follow. I danced to the music as it played.

The world was born for me. It was dying for me. It would end with my story embedded in its fabric. I was a letter in a word on a page of the only story that would ever truly matter. Without me, the word would be broken, and the sentence would be incomprehensible. The story would collapse.

I would never know how the story ended. I could never have that right. The time would come, though, when I would know. I would know when my body crumbled into a pile of ash. I would again become a part of the stars that birthed me. I would be infinitely connected to the cosmos. It is in that place that I would finally understand. Pierre knew and so would I.

I moved slowly to the music. I floated and spiraled on the moon's surface as white dust was kicked up from my movement. It surrounded me in a pale cloud.

I did not yet know how to live outside of myself. The Firebird showed me that it was possible to escape from the prison of my mind. She taught me that freedom was a beautiful reality.

The feathers in my hair flapped wildly as I moved.

Soon the tranquilizers would wear off and I would awaken in Meadowlark and be restrained for several days. My performance would come to an end. Yet, despite everything, it would not be long before they released me.

I had made my choice by not giving into the Beast. I would never know if it was the right one. I had seen visions of the past and the future. Yet neither existed. I knew that I was real on another plane. The blonde woman who had been murdered and left in the pond without a name, Seraphina and Poe, the aliens, The Doctor, the chickens from our farm, Pierre and Natasha, my parents, my sister, Aurora, the Beast, the white stag; they all lived somewhere within my veins. They flowed through me and I flowed through them - whether they wanted me there or not. I could never go back and change the things I had done. Fates and destinies are, perhaps, not as fixed as I would have had them.

I felt myself stop breathing as my dancing continued. Out of the corner of my eye, I watched Aurora lean forward.

Those futures I saw might have been as unalterable as my own death and birth. Yet, perhaps none of them would come to pass. The only thing I could do was exist.

The Beast thought he could own me. The Doctor thought he could own me. Seraphina thought she could own me. The white stag could have owned me, though the white stag would not have wanted that.

Perhaps the story does not itself know how it would end. If Maggie had not found me in the bathtub, I would have died that night. So many things could have turned out differently. If Aurora had used a thinner rope, it might have snapped. If she had selected a weaker branch, it might have given way. Her death was senseless, yet it was carved into the reality now. It was written into the story. No matter what, it had consequences that would always be felt. No one would ever know what might have happened if she had not died on that tree. Her death left markings on the story. My survival would leave markings as well. All that I knew was that I was alive. I had chosen to live.

I felt the song coming to a close as my performance reached its climax. I bent and twisted as the sensation came into my body. I allowed myself to loosen and be fluid.

I breathed heavily, bounding up as tears trickled down my cheek. I looked over to Aurora one last time and noticed that she wept, too.

Moondust flew up around me. My feathers floated up around my ears.

I had chosen to exist. I was once a supernova, and now all that was left was my core. I could either become a neutron star or a black hole.

I bounded upward off my toes and threw back my head and arms.

I felt the fluttering sensation of hope within me. The moths within my skull calmed and landed on my brain. They would sleep for a while, not forever, but for a while.

I closed my eyes as my grip on the moon began to fade. I knew where I would go, yet, at that moment, I was not afraid. At that moment, nothing on Heaven or Earth could have caged me. I was free, even though I did not yet have any idea what that would mean, or how long it would last. But I knew what freedom was. What a terrifying adventure it was to be.

I have existed. I exist. I will exist.

Epilogue

Tears were shed when Lily's ashes were released into the air. Her life had been long. Her body had been old. When her ashes were spread, most of them were taken by the wind and cradled within its arms.

All of those grains of her flew out to every corner of the planet, some traveled up into the sky and toward the atmosphere. Yet there was a single particle, a speckle of ash that may have been a portion of her pupil, or a piece of her lip, which landed on a blade of grass. It had clung to the ambivalent plant and had waited there.

Hours passed. The funeral was long over, and the mourners had gone. In that empty place, a herd of deer had passed through. One of the females who was heavily pregnant walked slower than the rest. When the rest of the herd stopped to graze, she allowed herself to relax.

She had eaten the blade of grass without care, without any understanding of what it was she ingested. It traveled down her throat easily. The grass and the last piece of what was once Lily fueled her in the most minute way. Only a short time passed before, without warning, a searing pain moved through her. She cried out, and the rest of the herb turned their heads to watch her. The warm summer wind had served as the deliverer. Some of the herd continued to graze, some watched and waited in anticipation, and others abandoned her.

She gave birth to a male. He was weak at first, gaining his strength after a few moments. That speck of ash was somewhere within him. It existed in his body, even though he had no idea of its existence. He would never understand. He would only know that he was alive, that he existed. As the years passed, he grew into a massive stag without a name. His hide was golden brown. His bellow was loud and echoing. He loved nothing more than basking in the glory of the sunshine while the rest of his herd grazed. His antlers were more beautiful than any other the wind had ever seen, with long fingers that reached up toward the sun.

Taylor Denton's work has appeared in Scribble, Coffin Bell Journal, and The Anti-Languorous Project. Her novella, The Mountain, was published through Running Wild Press in 2019. Denton grew up in Springfield, Missouri, and attended the University of Colorado - graduating with honors in 2020. She is currently working toward her MFA at Louisiana State University.

Running Wild Press publishes stories that cross genres with great stories and writing. RIZE publishes great genre stories written by people of color and by authors who identify with other marginalized groups. Our team consists of:

Lisa Diane Kastner, Founder and Executive Editor
Andrea Johnson, Acquisitions Editor, RIZE
Rebecca Dimyan, Editor
Andrew DiPrinzio, Editor
Cecilia Kennedy, Editor
Barbara Lockwood, Editor
Chris Major, Editor
Cody Sisco, Editor
Chih Wang, Editor
Benjamin White, Editor
Peter A. Wright, Editor
Lisa Montagne, Director of Education
Pulp Art Studios, Cover Design
Standout Books, Interior Design
Polgarus Studios, Interior Design
Nicole Tiskus, Production Manager Intern
Alex Riklin, Production Manager Intern
Alexis August, Production Manager Intern
Priya Raman-Bogan, Social Media Manager Intern

Learn more about us and our stories at www.runningwildpress.com

Loved this story and want more? Follow us at www.runningwildpress.com, www.facebook/runningwildpress, on Twitter @lisadkastner @RunWildBooks